Eclairs and Extortion

A Small Town Culinary Cozy Mystery

Maple Lane Cozy Mysteries
Book 5

C. A. Phipps

Dedication

I love and appreciate all my fans, and sometimes I'll offer the opportunity to appear in one of my books as a prize.

The winner of the Mother's Day - 'Why does your mom deserve to be in a book 2019' - was Ashlee Dolomore, who put her mom forward.

You'll find Dinah Dolomore appearing through the book as a new resident in the retirement community. Hopefully, she'll sound as lovely in this story as Ashlee says she is. :-)

Thanks to everyone who entered and to all the moms out there.

Cheryl x

Eclairs and Extortion

Marriage, Menace, and Murder!

Is it just coincidence that a body turns up in the park the same day Maddie's mom arrives in Maple Falls?

And who is the dark stranger wandering the streets of her hometown?

Preparations for a surprise seventieth birthday celebration for Gran are jeopardized when Maddie's part-time parent shows up unannounced. Devoted to her grandmother, Maddie won't allow her mom to ruin things the way she usually does.

With three generations at loggerheads, a murderer to find, and a party to organize, life is about to get crazy.

If you love your eclairs with a side of mystery, get your copy today!

C. A. Phipps

The Maple Lane Mysteries are light, cozy mysteries featuring a quirky cat-loving bakery owner who discovers she's a talented amateur sleuth.

5* Eclairs and Extortion is another delicious installment in the Maple Lane Mysteries."

Other books in The Maple Lane Mysteries

Sugar and Sliced - The Maple Lane Prequel
Book 1 Apple Pie and Arsenic
Book 2 Bagels and Blackmail
Book 3 Cookies and Chaos
Book 4 Doughnuts and Disaster
Book 5 Eclairs and Extortion
Book 6 Fudge and Frenemies
Book 7 Gingerbread and Gunshots
Book 8 Honey Cake and Homicide - preorder now!

Sign up for my new release mailing list and pick up a free recipe book!

Chapter One

Gran's seventieth birthday was going to be the party of the year. At least it would be in Maple Falls. With most of the residents likely to expect an invite, Madeline Flynn had her work cut out for her. Still, her darling grandmother deserved to have the best day possible.

So here they were on a glorious spring Sunday afternoon, brainstorming how to make it happen. Three of her closest friends sat in the upstairs apartment of Maddie's bakery, watching her tap her thigh anxiously, waiting for her to tell them how they could pull it off in two weeks.

The biggest problem, and there were several big ones, was trying to keep it a surprise. Small towns didn't tend to keep secrets very well, and Gran knew everyone from the mailperson to the mayor.

"Are you sure she'd want so many guests?" Suzy Barnes broke the silence.

The petite brunette was not only the local principal, she was also a town committee member and amazing at organizing events. Suzy was a great asset if the others agreed with her plans.

Angel laughed. "Everyone loves Gran, and those that don't can't help but admire her. They'll come if they get an invite, and I'm pretty sure even if they don't."

Angelina Broome was called Angel for a reason. A sweet southern girl who'd held on to her accent, she lit up the room with her bubbly personality. Maddie was grateful every day that Angel and her mom had moved here many years ago before Angel's mom remarried and moved to California.

Laura, the fourth member of the Girlz, the name they were known by since they were at school together, frowned. "We'll need a place big enough, and I can only think of the community center. Even that will be a stretch."

Laura had only been in town for just over a year, but she was one of them now. She was also Maddie's intern baker along with teenager Luke.

A large pad of paper, laptop, and various colored pens were lined up in an orderly fashion on the wooden coffee table. This was serious work, and they had limited time to get things sorted.

A few months back, Gran had informed them that she was not having any fuss on her birthday, and Maddie had decided to honor her wishes, because that's what she usually did.

Since that day, every person she met demanded a party take place, including Gran's dear friends, Jed Clayton and Mavis Anderson. They were incredibly upset, something she hadn't counted on. Their belief in Gran deserving a day to remember had Maddie turning full circle, making her dizzy with everything that needed to be done. Although, the short time frame of two weeks meant there would be less chance for the party information to be leaked.

"You're right about the center being a bit small, and with Gran being the chairperson of the community center committee, how are we going to keep a lid on this or even do the booking? She scrutinizes every piece of paper that comes to the committee," Maddie asked, fingers tapping once more.

A large ginger Maine coon looked up from where he lay curled on the biscuit-colored rug at her feet. Sensing her agitation, the intuitive feline jumped onto Maddie's lap. After nuzzling her chin and getting a reassuring hug, Big Red curled into a ball. She appreciated the moral support, if not the weight on her jeans-covered legs.

"We can't have a paper trail, apart from what the four of us do up here. Gran's too astute. We'll have to contact everyone by phone or in person. They can call us on our mobiles or at work to RSVP." Suzy scribbled on a pad.

Maddie shook her head. "That won't work at the bakery. Gran's sure to answer the phone on the days she works here."

Fit as a fiddle, Gran talked about reducing her days, but apart from Monday, her scheduled day off, and Tuesday afternoons when she had her community center meeting, the only compromise was leaving early the other days. It was definitely going to be hard to keep a lid on things.

"That's fine. They can contact me or Angel." Suzy made more notes.

"What about me? I don't mind fielding calls," Laura offered.

"You work here too. If she knows the caller and they ask for you instead of speaking to her, Gran will become suspicious. You're not a very good liar, sugar, but there'll be other ways you can help," Angel explained gently.

"She does have a suspicious nature." Maddie gave a smile that didn't reach her eyes. Another aspect had been bugging her since she decided to go ahead with the party. Of course, Angel noticed.

"Are you still feeling bullied into this?"

Maddie frowned. "Not bullied. I so want to make it a special day for Gran, but what if people show up just to ruin it?"

Laura was confused, but Angel and Suzy grimaced. It was Suzy who

addressed the elephant in the room.

"Do you mean your mom might come?"

Maddie nodded; a lump formed in her throat just thinking about it. Her mom did not do family get-togethers very well. In fact, not at all.

"But you are sending her an invitation, right?" Angel asked.

Maddie ran her fingers through ginger fuzz and sighed. "There's a couple of people I still can't decide about."

Suzy shook her head. "That won't do. We have two weeks to get this organized. So far we have a list of people to invite who will hardly fit in the one place that could possibly cope. We need to at least confirm who we're inviting so we know numbers."

Maddie leaned back on the white leather couch. "I know. Let's count those on the list already—definites and probables. As for Mom, well, it's a really hard decision to make."

"You know she probably won't come?" Angel mentioned gently.

"She didn't make any of my birthdays or graduation, but . . . ." Maddie broke off.

"Ava marches to a different drum and there is a chance she'll come for the heck of it," Suzy finished for her.

Maddie nodded. Her friends knew how her mom's leaving one day, rarely to return, upset her. But they couldn't truly appreciate the rejection she'd felt. With no other family to speak of, if it hadn't been for Gran and her late grandad taking her in, she might have ended up in care and taken away from Maple Falls.

She'd learned to live without a mom, but the idea that she could have missed out on the wonderful life she had made her shiver.

"Do you want my opinion?" Angel fluffed her long blonde hair, which fell around her shoulders in a cloud.

A hairdresser, Angel's hair was always immaculate. Unlike Maddie's, which when infrequently left out had a mind of its own, so she wore it braided and down her back. Cutting it was always on her mind, but Grandad had loved her hair and would brush it in the evenings before the fireplace. He made her swear to keep it like this. It had been when she was young, but she often heard his voice and remembered his wise words, and cutting her hair simply felt wrong.

Angel picked up Maddie's busy hand and stilled her fingers.

"Send the invite. You don't have to worry about whether she'll turn up if you think that she won't, but you will stop feeling guilty over not sending it. The result is something you have no control over, and you need to stop fretting."

Suzy and Laura nodded in agreement.

Maddie sighed. They were right. She'd given the

outcome too much importance and stupidly lost sleep over it. Her mom had a right to come, simple as that. "Okay. I'll do it."

Suzy ran the back of her hand dramatically across her forehead. "Phew! Now we can concentrate on the other stuff. Angel, you're in charge of decorations. Laura and Maddie, naturally the food falls to you."

Maddie handed her a sheet of paper. "This is the food list Laura and I made up. We think finger food is suitable and, more importantly, doable with Gran around. Laura and I will make the highlighted ones the night before. I'll ask Luke to help as well. He adores Gran and will definitely want to be involved."

It would take the three of them several hours to get the balance ready for so many people, but unless they could send Gran out for the Friday and keep her away on that Saturday, it was going to be tricky.

"The fact that we can't have a party without telling people when or where it's going to be held or who it's for is not helping. How can we approach that?" Laura asked.

Angel, who was beside Maddie on the couch, bounced a little on the sofa. Big Red glared. Angel kissed him by way of an apology. "Why don't we make it a mystery theme?"

"Oooh, I like that. What does that consist of?" Suzy's pen poised midair.

"We send out invites and a day but no venue, telling everyone not to mention it around town. Like a save the date. Jed can book the community center under the guise of something else and not tell that group anything."

"What about a family reunion?" Laura added.

Suzy nodded. "Excellent idea. How he'll keep it from Gran—I just don't know."

Maddie grimaced. "The poor man. He'll be hounded by

every silver-haired person for miles around who think they've been excluded from something major at the center, plus they'll all be wanting to know where Gran's party is."

"Personally, I love it, and I bet when it's revealed any upset will be quickly forgotten." Angel grinned.

"It might work. I don't like our chances, but we have to try." Maddie's fingers slowly unfurled from the lush fur on her lap. "Okay. I'll go talk to Jed tomorrow."

"We'd better call an end to this meeting and get down the road to the cottage before Gran sends out a search party." Angel began packing up the paper and pens.

Suzy stood and stretched. "As soon as you said that I became ravenous."

"I could eat." Maddie grabbed her bag and keys. "Ready when you are."

They rushed downstairs, jostling each other out the door. Laura appeared less enthusiastic about that, and Maddie assumed she was still coming to terms with the Girlz dynamics and physicality. Arm in arm, including Laura, they meandered down Plum Place with Big Red in their wake.

Chapter Two

Sunday dinner was a tradition in Maddie's family—an English one. To be fair, it was arguably held at lunchtime in that country, but Gran had her own rules and reasons why. Working hard on the farm, interspersed with feeding the family, she baked cakes and pies for whoever needed them, and her time was apportioned accordingly.

No matter what anyone was doing, come 6:00 p.m. they were expected front and center at the table with clean hands. Not that they were checked these days.

Big Red and all the Girlz were included in the standing invite, as was Maddie's boyfriend, Sheriff Ethan Tanner. They came if they could make it, which they did more often than not. Sometimes others would be invited, like Jed or Mavis. Tonight it was just the five of them.

Sitting down to roast chicken, potato salad, and all the trimmings, they were loading their plates when Big Red scampered down the hall from his spot under the table, anticipating a slight knock on the door.

Maddie rose, but the door opened before she took a

step. A familiar blonde woman walked in, pulling a case behind her. Closing the door, she came warily down the hall with Big Red close on her heels.

He dived under the table, while Maddie grabbed hold of the back of her chair to keep from falling. "Mom." It was the only word she could manage.

"Nice to see you too." Ava Flynn came into the room as though this was an everyday occurrence.

"W-w-what are you doing here?" Maddie stuttered.

Ava gave a tinkling laugh that sounded forced. "Can't a mother come home occasionally to see her only child? Or her mother?"

Dumbfounded, Maddie didn't know how to reply. Long ago, she'd decided that her mom felt a residual amount of guilt that made her come home at all, because Ava made no secret of the fact that she wasn't happy to be in Maple Falls.

The truth was, Ava rarely made it home for Christmas. Maybe once or twice. Years ago. And the year she first left, she stayed away for months.

Barely managing Christmas lunch, she hightailed it back to wherever she came from soon after they ate—as if one day was all she could manage. It tarnished an otherwise happy day, and though when she was young Maddie had cried for her mom, after that she understood that it was better this way.

Maddie had lost count of the towns and cities Ava had lived in and had no idea where she currently resided. It simply didn't matter once she got used to the idea that her mom didn't want to be part of their family in any meaningful way.

Besides, home had always been fractious when Ava Flynn was in it. Without her, Maddie's life was on an even keel. Now, old worries crashed down around her, and a hand slipped to her thigh to tap out her anxieties. Luckily Gran was not so discombobulated.

"Ava, you might have called, but now that you're here will you join us for dinner?"

Ava looked around at the faces. "I will if people will stop staring. You all act like you've seen a ghost."

"They're rare around here too," Suzy muttered as she laid another setting.

Ava narrowed her eyes for a second. "I didn't know an invitation was required these days, Mom."

Gran tutted. "Don't be silly, dear. This is your home and you're always welcome. I was only saying it would be nice to know you were coming."

Ava sniffed. "I didn't know myself until last night."

"We'll set another place. This is Laura. She's helping me around the farm as well as Maddie at the bakery."

Ava took a long look at Laura, who appeared to shrink under the intense gaze.

"That's nice," Ava said with no enthusiasm.

Maddie was incapable of doing more than resuming her seat. Angel pulled up another chair, placing it next to Gran. With a squeeze to Maddie's shoulder, Angel sat next to Ava so that Laura didn't have to.

"So where are you living now, Ms. Flynn?" Angel handed Ava the plate of crispy roast chicken.

Nonchalantly, Ava took a piece. "Blackwell."

"Sorry?" Angel frowned.

Ava helped herself from the other dishes she could reach. "I'm Mrs. Blackwell now."

Angel gasped, and Maddie tried to keep the hurt from her face. She knew she'd failed, because Laura made a soothing sound from across the table.

"You got married?" Suzy looked horrified before giving Maddie a searching look.

Ava raised an eyebrow at the group in general. "I see that surprises everyone?"

Like Angel, Suzy wasn't intimidated by Ava's haughtiness. She also liked to get to the point without too much prevarication.

"A little. I distinctly remembering you telling us when we were a good deal younger that marriage wasn't necessary."

Gran made a rude noise. "How could you talk to them that way?"

Ava had the grace to look embarrassed.

"Suzy," Angel admonished. "Mrs. Blackwell will want to talk to Gran and Maddie about this later."

Ava took the salad from Gran and slapped some on her plate. "Not really."

"Let's just eat," Maddie told them, passing gravy to her mom while her mind spun like a hamster on a wheel.

Whatever Ava was here for it couldn't be the birthday party since she hadn't got an invitation yet. Maddie could find a little relief in that. The problem was that Ava had a talent for causing trouble, and if she wasn't going to be pleasant to Gran, then Maddie did not want her here. Not even for a day.

This insight made her realize how much she'd come to terms with potentially not seeing her mom again. Her friends looked just as perturbed, and without their usual chatting and banter, dinner was an awkward affair.

Laura didn't utter a word, watching openmouthed when Suzy threw Ava some attitude. Incredibly loyal to her friends, Suzy was used to dealing with the odd irate parent and bratty child, but poor Laura, though having come a long way from the bullied woman who'd come to town over a year ago, was still wary of any altercations and didn't like to be around them if she could avoid it.

As the time ticked by—literally, thanks to the grandfather clock in the lounge—Maddie's anger rose. Ava had no right to make any of them feel uncomfortable. She was the outsider here and had said so herself on more than one occasion while she harassed Gran and Grandad.

When Laura, Suzy, and Angel could no longer pretend they were enjoying the meal, Maddie put down her knife and fork, taking a deep breath. "Would you all mind going home now? Gran and I will handle the dishes."

They stood as one, palpable relief swirling around the three women. So different in looks, Angel tall and blonde, Suzy short and dark-haired, and Laura average height and redheaded, they were amazing friends and would have stayed if she'd asked.

"Are you sure? I could tidy up first?" Laura sidled to the door.

"No need. We've got this," Maddie told her with fake optimism.

Angel gave a disbelieving glance before they left, and Maddie knew she would have to give them a debrief tomorrow.

Meanwhile, Ava smirked as she used corn bread to wipe up the last of her gravy, as if she hadn't had a meal in weeks.

"Are you done?" Gran asked her with a degree of censure.

"What, no dessert?" Ava adopted a look of mock horror.

Gran stared for a moment. "If you want some apple pie, it's in the kitchen."

The tone was enough to warn anyone that they were

perilously close to Gran's line in the sand. She was usually an amazing host, but would only take so much rudeness.

Ava sat back, eyes calculating. "Things have really changed, although you're still a great cook."

"That's the first time you've told me that," Gran said with surprise.

"Really? I'm sure I never said otherwise."

Ava was being intentionally argumentative, because Maddie remembered her mother refusing to eat sometimes when it wasn't what she wanted. It was time to nip this passive-aggressive behavior in the bud.

"What do you want here, Mom?"

Eyes the same deep blue as Maddie's and Gran's narrowed. "Didn't I tell you to call me Ava?"

Maddie shrugged. "You did, but you'll have to excuse me if I sometimes forget."

"Still sassy, I see." Ava turned to Gran. "You've spoiled her. I told you that's what would happen."

"Please don't talk to Gran like that. She's been an awesome role model," Maddie said tersely.

Ava scowled. "I don't think you get to tell me how to talk to my own mother. We have a different relationship to you and her, as you well know."

"We are all well aware of the regard you have for your father and me," Gran said evenly, crossing her arms.

Ava flinched. "I didn't mean anything by that, and I didn't come here to argue."

Gran leaned forward. "Well, you could have fooled me. Now get to the point and tell us what you want."

For the first time, Ava looked unsure of herself. "It's tricky."

Gran and Maddie waited, their patience stretching along with the silence. It was obviously going to be bad.

Maddie's stomach flipped a few times while Ava seemed to be weighing up what she was going to say. Or how she was going to say it. Eventually, she looked up, and unexpectedly, her mouth quivered.

"My husband isn't well. He was poisoned."

Maddie gasped. "Poisoned? Then why aren't you with him?"

"They think I did it." Fear slipped over Ava's worry.

"Who are 'they'? The police?" Gran demanded.

Ava chewed her lip for a moment. "Yes. But only because his family put the idea into their heads. They're rich and they think I want to kill him for his money. They wouldn't let me near him."

Her mom was naturally upset, but intrigue fought Maddie's empathy for Ava, and she leaned closer when Gran asked, "You're married and obviously weren't arrested, so how could they stop you?"

Ava shuddered. "William was terribly sick and in hospital. On the second day I was told they had proof it was me and that if I came near him they'd have me arrested."

"Why do they assume you're guilty of poisoning him?" Maddie asked.

"The brothers had an argument. I may have said something along the lines of he should drop dead. I didn't mean it and I didn't say it to William. People say that all the time and it doesn't mean a thing. Unfortunately, his brother won't concede that. He was also the only other person around and as far as I'm concerned the only one with a motive." Ava shifted in her chair.

Maddie sucked in a breath. "Exactly how dangerous is his family?"

"His brother is pretty scary," Ava admitted. "He never liked me from the start, and he belittles William." Her voice

17

rose in anger. "I don't know how I can fix this from here, but I need your help, Maddie."

Gran's voice rose as her palm slapped the table. "You want Maddie to be involved in something that might endanger her?"

Ava glared at her mom. "Spare me the outrage. I've heard how she's the queen sleuth around Maple Falls. Maddie can take care of herself. Dad made sure of it. And don't pretend you don't know the things she's capable of."

Gran glared right back. "Your father might have taught her a few things to keep her safe, but Maddie shouldn't have to deal with whatever you've embroiled yourself in."

"I knew you wouldn't understand, but you are my family. You're supposed to help," Ava said stubbornly.

"And you're old enough to get yourself out of trouble without our help." Gran stood and began collecting plates.

It was Ava's turn to gasp. "You're turning me away?"

"You can stay the night and leave in the morning." Gran nodded to the stairs. "Your room is the same."

"I'll put sheets on the bed when I've done the dishes," Maddie offered, relieved that it was just for one night. Relieved she wouldn't be subjected to more argument. Although that might be a little premature.

Ava stood, knocking her chair against the wall, her eyes dark. "I can't believe you two. I knew you'd gang up on me, but I didn't think you'd shun me like everyone else."

"And we can't believe you. Ignoring us for years. Us never being good enough. Until now. And we never shunned you!" Maddie stormed into the kitchen and began none too gently to wash dishes, hoping desperately that Ava would go without a fuss as soon as it was daylight and they could return to normal. Which meant not having to worry about what Ava might have brought to town along with her animosity.

"You okay, sweetheart?" Gran said gently as she placed more dishes on the counter. "Your mom's gone to her room."

Maddie blew away a strand of hair that had escaped the braid. "Yes. What about you?"

"I'm fine."

It was clear from their voices and hunched shoulders that they were both lying, and they shared a sad smile.

"She's scared, that's why your mom's here. I don't know if what she says is the truth or partly exaggeration, but if she'd come here with a better attitude I'd have welcomed her with open arms."

Maddie grimaced. "Despite everything?"

Gran nodded. "Because we're family and do our best to forgive. Everybody makes mistakes, and you can never tell if wisdom will win. Hopefully, she'll feel differently tomorrow."

Maddie was skeptical about any change to her mom's attitude. "Why can't she see how she hurts us?"

"I don't know, sweetheart. Still, she's my daughter. I brought her into this world, and you can't forget a thing like that."

"Or that she's my mom," Maddie added wryly. Many times she'd wished that Gran and Grandad were her real parents, and in most ways they had been. Unfortunately, that hadn't stopped her from also wishing for her mom to come back home and have things be the way she imagined a family should be.

Gran and Maddie talked softly, working in unison, the way they always did. They'd discovered problem-solving worked better this way, and with Maddie's foray into amateur sleuthing, they'd had their share of them. This was of course more personal, apart from when Big Red had been kidnapped last year.

Despite the friction, Maddie couldn't help worrying for her mom, and she knew Gran felt it too. "Do you think she's safe here?"

Gran placed the dried plates on the dresser. "I want to believe that she is, because if not, then potentially neither are we. Which reminds me, where's our sheriff tonight?"

Maddie blushed. Ethan was away in Destiny. The larger town to the north was holding a hot rod show and most of the department was helping out in case the boy racers got out of hand, as they were capable of doing.

She explained, adding, "He'll be back in the morning."

Gran nodded. "Good. Maybe he could swing by tomorrow when he gets back."

"Do you mean so that we can tell him about Mom even though she's leaving?"

Gran looked a little cagey. "It's always nice to have him back in town, but yes. Regardless of where she is, for my own peace of mind, he could look into this Blackwell man and tell us if he or his family are the kind of people we should worry about."

Maddie dried her hands. "I think I should stay the night. Just in case."

"No, you get home. Big Red likes his own bed."

The ginger Maine coon heard his name and came out from under the table where he'd been hiding from the raised voices. He yawned and stretched, then padded to the door. On his way, he looked up the staircase, his ears pinned back. Did he know that Ava didn't like cats? They had never met before today, but Big Red was very astute and had stayed well away from her.

Gran smiled. "The boss has spoken. Plus, I'm sure

Laura will be back soon, or perhaps you could call her and say the coast is clear?"

Although Laura lived with Gran, staying in Maddie's old room, she'd escaped the confrontation with the others. No doubt she'd gone to Angel's. When Angel had gone through a rough patch with her ex-husband, Laura kindly stayed there for a while, but she loved the cottage and Gran. Maddie knew Laura would come back here in a heartbeat to keep Gran safe.

"I'll do that on my way home." She kissed Gran's cheek.

It was useless to protest, and she let herself out with a heavy heart—which nearly stopped when a figure rose from Grandad's old chair on the porch.

Chapter Three

"Laura! You gave me a fright. Why are you out here?" Maddie reined in a yell while her heart hammered in her chest.

Startled, Laura grabbed the wooden bannister to stop herself falling backwards, the whites of her eyes huge in the semidarkness. "Sorry. I didn't want to leave Gran, but you all needed time so I thought I'd wait until you were done."

Maddie smiled gratefully. "Thank you, but you live here. Please don't ever think you have to leave this house because of my mom."

Feeling guilty for Laura being out here on her own, Maddie couldn't help the fact that having Laura back in the cottage gave her peace of mind. Now that Maddie lived above her bakery, it meant that Gran was never alone. That mattered even more tonight, with Ava in the house. Mother and daughter they might be, but Ava didn't treat Gran with the respect she deserved.

Laura sniffed the air in appreciation. "I didn't mind being out here. It's so peaceful. With the fields on one side and the shops and your bakery just down the street on the other, it feels like the best of all worlds."

Maddie understood completely. "It is beautiful. Sometimes I can't believe I worked in New York for so long. I learned a lot and it's a fascinating city, but Maple Falls is home."

Laura stepped fully into the light. "Is it weird that I feel the same way after such a short time?"

Maddie recognized the look on her friend's face. Being unsure of where you belonged was not as rare as it should be. "Not to me. Home is different for everyone, and you fit in here like the rest of us. You're one of the Girlz now. It's as simple as that."

Laura sniffed in a different way. "I'm so grateful to have found you all and that you let me in to your group."

Laura's sincerity was touching and warmed Maddie's heart. "And we're grateful that you decided to stay."

Laura ducked her head. "I really hope things work out with your mom."

"I do too, but there are no guarantees. I'll see you in the morning."

She heard a certain stiffness in her voice and wished she didn't react this way. It was one of the side effects of talking about Ava in any capacity. Hopefully Laura wouldn't have to endure more of her mom's toxicity.

Big Red trotted beside her as they walked down Plum Place to the back of the shops. Each of the four in this block had their own small garden, and Maddie's was overflowing with vegetables, herbs, fruit, and flowers. Opening the small gate attached to the low stone wall, Maddie continued up the path that led into the bakery kitchen.

She dropped her bag and keys on the table, an urge to hit something or have a rant about bad timing bubbling within her. Either would achieve nothing but might make her feel better.

With a rueful smile at her white knuckles, she fed Big Red, then went upstairs to the apartment. Sleep wasn't possible, so she decided to work on the lists for the party. Usually she'd bake something, but this was a better use of her time, because she was determined more than ever to give Gran a day to remember.

Getting comfortable on the couch with laptop, pen, paper, and Big Red snuggled up beside her, Maddie tried to concentrate. She loved the cottage dearly, after all, it was where she'd grown up, but her bakery and apartment filled her with peace or energy, depending on what she needed at the time. Her faithful cat was the other calming influence. Kissing his head, she checked the lists for who they had already tagged for an invite and who they had overlooked.

There was family—not as many as there could be, since Grandad's side ended with his passing and Gran had emigrated from England as a young woman. She did have a brother back there who had a son, but it was too short notice for them to come over, even if they were able to. The airfares were horrendous and it was a long way to travel.

Which left Maddie and her mom. The Girlz—Suzy, Angel, and Laura—counted as family, even if they were no blood relation, and Suzy's parents were also included in that list.

Friends—this was the tricky one. Jed Clayton and Mavis Anderson were the closest ones. In fact, Maddie had long suspected that Jed hoped for something more than friendship, but she figured at turning seventy, Gran wasn't willing to make any changes to her full life.

The community center had all sorts of things happening, and with Gran the chairperson of the center committee, she helped out with most groups. Therefore, every member could claim to be her friend.

Then there was the country club, whose members would also expect an invite. They had a great deal of respect for Gran, who'd instigated, as only she could do, the opposing factions of the community center and country club finding a peaceful coexistence. Before that, there had been a horrible divisiveness.

Last, but no means least, were all the people around town who Gran knew from when she'd arrived as a young bride, plus any new people she'd taken a shine to. There were nearly as many on this list, and only with Jed and Mavis's help and by talking to people coming into the bakery had the Girlz been able to put full names to most of those.

The spreadsheet was expanding, and Maddie didn't have a clue how they could possibly fit everyone into the community center. Frustrated, she pulled up a map of Maple Falls on her laptop. There had to be somewhere that had facilities and space to put a large tent . . . .

And there it was!

Slapping her forehead, Maddie groaned. They'd been so focused on having it at the community center or some-where in town, they'd completely forgotten about Maple Fields. It had been donated to the town by the very first mayor and was where all the markets and festivals were held. The land there would be perfect. Close to town, it wasn't too far to travel to.

It had built-in restrooms with plenty of toilets and a large flat area where the huge tent was usually positioned for judging the cakes and produce at the spring festival.

Her phone beeped—it was Ethan leaving a message.

Hey, girlfriend. Remember me? I'm outside and see your light's on. Want company?

YES! she replied before throwing the phone on the couch and racing down the stairs to unlock the door and yank it open. Ethan stood outside, and she threw herself into his arms.

He kissed the top of her head and chuckled. "What did I do to deserve such a welcome? I'll try to do it more often."

She smiled into his jacket, inhaling the familiar scent of her sheriff. Warm and masculine, it washed over her. Being in his arms was enough to make her feel safe. From what, she wasn't sure, but she felt the world had shifted and that it hadn't stopped since her mom arrived.

"Just being here. That's all you need to do," she mumbled.

He put a hand under her chin and tipped it so he could look into her eyes. "What's wrong?"

His concern warmed her, but the words were stuck, and the smile she tried for clearly fell short.

"Now I'm really worried," he said. "Let's get inside."

Once they were upstairs, Ethan dropped his hat on the kitchen counter and led her to the sofa.

Maddie curled her legs beneath her, and he sat beside her, waiting patiently while she sucked in a couple of big breaths. "Mom's in town."

He frowned. "Ava's here?"

She nodded, not trusting her voice further. Ethan knew all about Ava Flynn, as did the rest of the town. She was viewed as argumentative, flighty, and the cause of scandal. Her mom had hurt Gran and Grandad with her inability to stay away from the rough crowd who came to town and stayed one summer. If that wasn't bad enough, she'd eloped with one of them. He'd run off, leaving her with a baby. You couldn't hide the facts in a small town.

As much as it hurt, Ava moving away had brought their small family some much needed peace. The gossip eventually died down, and Maddie was able to deal with any snide comments with the help of the Girlz. And Ethan.

"Tea?"

Not waiting for an answer, Ethan went to the small kitchen that Maddie hardly used because of the bakery's one downstairs.

With Gran being British, tea was considered a staple and drunk several times a day. Possibly more in times of need. This definitely qualified.

She took the cup and saucer with a smile and sipped. "That's not bad at all, Sheriff."

"I'm a quick learner. Just one of my many talents." He raised an eyebrow. "Now, do you want to talk about Ava, or shall we discuss something that will make you feel better?"

"I'd be happy to talk about anything else, but it's difficult to get my mind off it." Maddie sighed. "Mom's in trouble. How much is unknown. She wants to stay at the cottage for an unspecified length of time, but Gran's asked her to leave tomorrow."

Ethan whistled. "That must have been hard for her. Ava's her daughter, after all."

Maddie grimaced. "She seemed fine when I left. But you're right. Gran will be feeling guilty about sending Mom away, even though she shouldn't."

Ethan screwed up his face. "I suppose it's man trouble?"

Maddie nodded, unable to take offence. "No surprises there, but she actually married this one."

"Wow! I did not see that coming." He shook his head, lifting his mug of coffee.

"Me either, but there's more. Apparently, there's an issue with him potentially being poisoned. His family believe Mom to be responsible."

Ethan choked on his drink, spraying the liquid across a disgruntled Big Red, who'd earlier forced his way between them without any intervention.

"Sorry, boy." Ethan dabbed at him with tissues he grabbed from the table, and Big Red took a swipe at his hand, which Ethan quickly retracted. "Do they have evidence that she was involved?"

"None that I know of, but to be honest, we didn't discuss anything in detail. And Mom's very cagey about most things."

"I daresay it was shock enough to have her turn up out of the blue," Ethan sympathized, as Big Red began to clean himself.

Grateful that Ethan understood how her mother's unexpected arrival upset her, Maddie smiled weakly and handed him more tissues for his shirt. "That's exactly how it was. We were having dinner, and she came into the cottage as if it was the most normal thing in the world. I just don't get why she'd come here."

"I'm sorry you have to deal with this. I know how fraught the relationship with your mom is. Clearly she thinks home is the best place for her right now."

"I guess."

He took her hand. "Can I help in any way?"

She smiled. "Having you here is a good start, but I'm glad you asked. Would you check on her husband and see if he or his family could hurt anyone?"

"You mean Ava?"

Maddie tapped her thigh. "No matter how Mom is, I

29

couldn't bear it if she was hurt through me not taking her cry for help seriously."

"If her husband's family has the capacity to poison one of their own or if Ava was actually the target, then you can't simply send her on her way. Anyway, you look tired. I should go and let you get some sleep. If you're feeling any better?"

"I am, but I'm not sure how I'll get to sleep."

"Shall I make you some hot milk?"

Maddie managed a short laugh. "Look at you, being all domestic. Maybe I should try a hot bath first. Besides, you must be tired as well; you've had some long days lately."

"You're not wrong. I promise to get on to it first thing tomorrow." He stood, stretching and letting out a loud yawn. His shirt tugged against his shoulders and chest. Then he pulled her to her feet and into his arms. "I don't like to see you so upset."

Small lines appeared around his eyes. It was nice to have him around, knowing he cared, but she didn't want him to worry so much. "Maybe I'm overreacting and the situation is not as serious as Ava painted it to be."

He nodded. "Let's hope so."

Then he kissed her, and Maddie could have stayed in his arms all night where it was safe and peaceful, their hearts beating in unison.

Chapter Four

Monday morning brought sunshine a few hours after Maddie was woken by a grumpy cat.

Big Red had slapped her on the arm. More than once. Not having slept well, it was later than usual when Maddie stumbled out of bed to fix his breakfast.

With that attended to, she had a quick shower and hurriedly dressed. Not wanting to leave Gran with Ava for too long and with a desire to make sure her mom actually left, Maddie didn't stop for breakfast. However, there were several things to do before she could in all good conscience leave.

The oven was on and bread set to rise by the time Laura and Luke arrived. She felt that was a good start. After a brief explanation for Luke's benefit, the questions began.

"All I can say is that I don't have any answers. Mom turned up unexpectedly, and she says she's in trouble. I need to help Gran deal with her, so I'd appreciate the two of you helping me out the way you always do."

"We're happy to," Laura said, and Luke nodded emphatically.

A large whiteboard had lists for the day as well as individual ones so that they could ensure everything was covered. Knowing her team was more than capable of getting the shelves in the food cabinet close to full by the time she returned was a blessing.

Walking down Plum Place to the cottage, passing the fields and the back of the shops, was usually a pleasant thing to do. Not this morning—even with Big Red for company. As much as she liked to think positively, there was simply far too much history to do so today, and the closer she got, the more anxiety built inside her like a layer cake.

Looking like it came straight off a chocolate box, the white cottage had both wisteria and bougainvillea wrapped around the front porch. Spring in Maple Falls was Maddie's favorite time of year and she paused to sniff at the air, appreciating that as delightful as the fragrances were, this was a delaying tactic, and eventually forced herself to step inside.

Ava sat at the table with Gran—the tension palpable. Maddie understood without being told that things were not going according to plan. Or perhaps they were, but only to the one Ava had.

"You're not leaving this morning?" Maddie asked bluntly.

Ava shook her head. "It's not safe for me to go to William just now."

"Why?" Maddie flinched at her own tone. Respect had been drummed into her, but if she didn't ask in a direct way, her mother was not likely to answer—or sidle right past it.

Ava took a deep breath. "I heard he thinks he's being watched."

"By whom? His family?" Maddie pressed.

"I don't want to talk about it." Ava turned away slightly.

Maddie tried a different approach. "You'll have to tell us if you know more, otherwise we can't help you—I can't help you."

Ava's face contorted, and her hands rubbed together as if she were cold. "It's not that easy. If I tell you, then the danger for both of you could be worse."

Gran folded her arms. "Yet you came home and potentially brought these dangers with you."

Ava stood, hands on hips. "You can't seriously think I wanted to come back to this town? I know what people think of me. If I had a choice, I wouldn't have."

Gran's eyes widened. "Yes, dear. We know where we and Maple Falls stand in your esteem, but if your husband is so ill, you should be with him. So, who exactly are you hiding from and why would they be searching for you?"

Ava's hands resumed their twisting. "It's William's brother, Nicholas. He wants the family's house in England."

"Ava, that doesn't help. Sit down and start from the beginning. Please." Gran insisted.

Ava sighed and dropped heavily into the chair. "William is the eldest of the two. When his parents passed away, he was given their estate in Devon, England."

"You said house, and now it's an estate," Maddie noted.

With a pained expression, Ava mumbled, "And a castle."

Maddie whistled. "You own a castle?"

"I don't own anything. It's William's," Ava said firmly.

"But aren't you married?" Maddie asked.

"Yes," Ava reluctantly admitted.

"Carry on, dear," Gran said.

Ava clasped her hands together. "Like I said, William as the eldest inherited the estate, then just before he came to

California, his uncle passed away and he inherited the castle. Nicholas is under the impression that's why I married his brother. He said terrible things to me about being a gold digger, and the next thing, William is poisoned. William and I believe from their line of questioning that the police have me pegged as the main suspect. I don't think Nicholas would say anything to change their mind."

"So now the police are after you as well as the family? You never told us how serious this was yesterday." Wide-eyed, Maddie struggled to take in all the information. Suspected poisoning, and now a castle?

Ava shrugged, but her voice shook. "I didn't want to leave him, but William begged me to get out of the city. He was feeling much better, but Nicholas insisted he remain in hospital for another day as per the doctor's recommendation. William had this idea in his head that if we separated, the truth would come out somehow, exonerating me. The only reason I did go was that he hired a bodyguard to protect him."

Maddie tapped her thigh for a moment. "Is this the person keeping you up to date?"

Ava nodded. "I worked with Jerry Sims at a bar. I trust him as I do William's cousin, Marcus. By the way, I didn't tell anyone else where I was going except for William."

Gran tutted. "Is that supposed to make us feel safe, dear? Surely anyone with a little common sense would look to your family for your whereabouts?"

Ava's cheeks flushed. "Not if they knew our history, which Nicholas seems to have uncovered."

Maddie's teeth clenched. There it was; their dysfunctional family was out in the open once more. She turned to Gran. "I'll get Ethan to stop by later. He'll know what to do about this."

"I don't want you telling anyone," Ava said shortly.

Confused, Maddie explained, "Ethan Tanner is the sheriff in Maple Falls."

Ava shook her head. "I don't care who he is. It's bad enough that your friends were here last night. No one else needs to know I'm here."

Maddie's fingers tapped almost painfully on her thigh. "That's too bad, since I've already told him you're here and gotten him to look into your new family."

"How dare you!"

Gran placed a fresh teapot on the table with a little bang. "That's enough, Ava. If you're willing to have us involved, then you have to accept that we'll be trying to protect ourselves as well as you."

"Besides, if the police are looking for you, then this will surely be the first place they'll look? Ethan can facilitate that." Maddie opted for a softer approach, which seemed to work. "You did ask for my help. This is it."

Ava seemed to shrink. "I need some time to figure this out. The bodyguard will keep me updated about William and when he'll be released. I heard this morning that the police have finished questioning everyone, which Jerry says is protocol in cases like this. He was trained in security and knows things like this." She paled. "However, they do want to talk to me again."

Gran folded her arms. "I'm sure they do if you're the chief suspect, which is precisely why Ethan needs to know. He is dating your daughter, and that might put him in a very bad situation if he doesn't let anyone know."

Maddie was confused. "Who is left to hurt your husband if you've ruled out yourself and Nicholas? You mentioned his family blamed you."

Ava squirmed. "I really meant Nicholas. William's

bodyguard assured me that apart from his brother, no one has been to visit William since I left yesterday. If Nicholas is behind this, I can't believe he would be so stupid as to do anything while William is being so closely watched."

Ava was a hard person to get details from. "What happens when he gets out of hospital?"

"I've organized to secretly have him brought to Destiny. William's cousin will hire a room there. Marcus brought me that far, and I got the taxi driver to drop me in town."

"That would be Bernie. I'll have a word with him so he knows not to tell anyone of your whereabouts." Gran left the table to make the call, allowing them all a respite to gather their thoughts.

Another knock at the door gave Maddie an excuse to also leave the room. Nervous, she had an urge to yell out "friend or foe," but that seemed ridiculous. Especially when she saw the tall sheriff on the porch.

Ethan's lovely smile instantly faded.

"It's not going well?" he asked as he entered.

She sighed. "Quite frankly, the situation is a mess, and there's more to the story than I imagined. You better come and talk some sense into her."

Coming face-to-face with a pale Ava, Ethan was courteous. He held out a hand. "Pleased to meet you again."

Ava stared at him for a moment before taking the proffered hand. "So, you're the sheriff? I seem to recall a skinny kid hanging around Madeline. That's you, isn't it?"

The tips of Ethan's ears turned pink. "It is. I like to think it was a mutual thing. Like it is now."

He gave Maddie a wink.

She flushed a little at the memory of the young couple who couldn't agree on their future. A major argument made the subsequent move to New York City to pursue her career easier. She looked at her mom. Change was possible.

Ava raised an eyebrow. "So you two really are a thing again?"

"He's my boyfriend," Maddie said defensively. Her mom had never approved of any of her friends, and Maddie didn't expect anything to change in that regard. Hope had been a fleeting thing, after all.

"I guess with your propensity for finding trouble, it must be quite handy to have a sheriff on hand." Ava smirked.

Maddie gasped. "What do you mean by that?"

"Even Maple Falls gets a little airtime and space in the papers around elections and festivals. Your name's been mentioned a few times in connection with some crimes. That sealed the deal for me to come here," Ava stated.

Stunned, Maddie clasped her hands together. Her mother was keeping tabs? A funny feeling in her stomach began to expand. The perception that Ava had no idea about her daughter's life was losing a little traction. It was a little scary to have things put in question that previously were a certainty.

Suddenly, Maddie had a moment of clarity. Her mom was clever. At least, she probably thought she was. She'd turned the conversation to Maddie and away from this serious matter. Did she not understand that this was the only way?

With her emotions running rampant, Maddie sighed heavily. "You need to tell Ethan everything you've told Gran and me. Otherwise you'll probably end up in jail."

Ava grimaced, giving Ethan a worried glance. Several heartbeats later, she nodded. "All right, but it can't go any further."

Ethan remained silent on that point, and Ava fussed with her blouse. Maddie assumed she was buying time while she made up her mind about what to divulge and gave her a pointed look before helping Gran in the kitchen.

Whether she finally understood or not, when they were all sitting and had a cup of tea or coffee, Ava's reluctance slipped far enough to give Ethan the full picture. Or as full as Maddie and Gran were given.

Ethan had removed his notebook from one of the many pockets of his uniform and scribbled in it several times before asking questions. "Do you know when your husband will arrive in Destiny?"

"He could be on his way now. He intended on slipping out when the doctor had done her rounds," Ava told them sheepishly.

Maddie and Gran looked at each other in wonder at the new information.

"Will he be staying here?" Ethan asked.

"There's a hotel room booked for him and his body-guard in Destiny," Ava stated.

Ethan didn't give that idea any credence. "It would be a good idea to have everyone in one place for now. That way I can keep an eye on the cottage, because like it or not, this will be the first place to look. I'll also contact the Destiny Police Department."

Ava shook her head. "I don't think you should be spreading the details. William insisted I keep this as quiet as possible."

"I'm sorry, but I don't have a choice, and actually neither do you. It's more than likely since you fled the city that you will be regarded as suspicious. To clear your name, the police department there will need some assurance that you aren't dangerous," Ethan told her.

"The wife is always the first suspect, right?"

Ava sounded sad, and for the millionth time Maddie wished she knew what made her mom tick. She was as complicated today as she'd always been, it was so hard to gauge her sincerity or whether she spoke truthfully.

Ethan nodded. "Often, she is. However, the police never rest on one suspect when things aren't clear, and usually even if they seem to be."

"I think it's more than clear that I couldn't do something like this, but I don't have the same influence as William's brother." A shrillness crept into Ava's voice, tinged with frustration. "That's why William made me go. He finally realized that Nicholas isn't fond of me."

"What do you mean by influence? Over whom?" Ethan's pen poised over the notebook.

Ava shrugged. "Nicholas knows important people and has money. A great deal of it, I believe. I'm a penniless nobody. It's obvious who would be believed if he said I poisoned my husband."

"Would he know about poisons?" Ethan asked casually, not commenting on whether it was obvious or not.

Ava's mouth gaped for a moment. "I never thought Nicholas actually poisoned William. I just assumed he could afford to hire someone to do it."

"I understand that you feel aggrieved by your husband's brother but nothing you've said would lead anyone to feel assured that he tried to murder his brother. We need evidence."

She jumped to her feet. "It had to be him! Except I believe he wanted to murder me."

Gran made a soothing sound. "Calm down, dear. We're not saying we disbelieve you."

Arms crossed, she looked mutinously at them. "It sure sounds like it."

Maddie put a hand on her mother's. It was the first touch for both of them in several years, and they both stared at the point of contact. It did feel strange, and Ava chewed her lip, looking unsure of what she should do.

"We'll get to the bottom of this. You need to trust us. Trust Ethan." Maddie spoke gently and moved her hand.

Ava took her seat again and took a deep breath. "You'll really let me stay and help me?"

"Of course. We're family." Gran poured tea matter-of-factly.

It was obvious to the rest of them that Gran and Maddie couldn't let Ava flounder alone in this convoluted mystery, but Ava looked bewildered.

Maddie could imagine that coming home to hide had seemed like a good plan, albeit the only one her mom might have come up with. No doubt it grated that she had to ask her daughter to sift through the clues and to ask for a place to stay. The fact that she and Gran were willing to help, despite being upset at her underhandedness, must indeed feel implausible.

Meekly Ava answered more questions about the bodyguard and William's cousin, but there really wasn't much she could add.

Chapter Five

Maddie walked Ethan to the door and then on down the path to the road. He pulled her under the maple tree that grew on Gran's property but hung over the fence and gave them some privacy from the cottage. Ethan shook his head, taking her hands in his.

"Your mom's not in a good position. Running away from an investigation is pretty serious. I've given the investigator my word that Ava will not leave town and will be available for further questioning."

Maddie sighed. "I imagined it would be more involved than she thought. You've seen and heard her, so you must know that whatever we've said to persuade her to come out into the open met with deaf ears?"

"Of course I do. Your mom's stubborn. She is, after all, a Flynn, and I do recollect how she was before leaving town."

His wry grin drew an answering one to her lips. Her mom was naturally upset, but perhaps this was all a storm in a teacup, since Ava was prone to dramatic statements and had always been excitable. Still, a poisoning did occur and somebody was responsible.

"What can we do now?"

"Nothing at this moment. I'm sure you have to get back to the bakery and I'll head back to the station and see what else I can find out about the family and how the investigation is going in California."

She nodded, tamping down any impatience. "I appreciate that this is tricky for you, Ethan, and thanks for treating Mom so gently."

He kissed the tip of her nose. "You don't have to thank me. Your mom's nearly family, after all."

Maddie suppressed a grin. "Why, Sheriff, I don't know what you mean."

He snorted. "Yeah, you do. But that's a conversation for another time." Then he kissed her.

Slow and long, ending more passionately than it began, it took her breath away. This was clearly his intention, as he gave her a cheeky grin, then sauntered back to his car.

With a slow smile, Maddie watched him walk away, forgetting for a moment the reason for this early morning meeting. Big Red meowed at her feet, snapping her out of fog land, and together they speed walked to the bakery.

"You know, I'm pretty sure Ethan is getting ready to fix a date. What do you think, boy?"

The ginger fluff ball looked up at her and honest to goodness winked, his tail doing a dance around his back and smacking her on the leg.

She chuckled. "Good. I'd hate to think I imagined it!"

Talking to Big Red made her feel good and often led to an answer she'd been searching for. Who was to say if it was simply the process or her cat's common sense that supplied it?

At the bakery, as predicted, everything was well underway, and Luke was in the process of opening up the shop. The first customer of the day was Angel. No surprises there.

"Morning. How are you doing, sugar? Is your mom gone?" she called to Maddie in the kitchen.

Maddie slipped on her crisp white apron emblazoned with Maple Lane Bakeries on the front and came through the opening. No one else was in the shop, so she quietly told her best friend what was happening.

Angel chewed her lower lip for a moment, and Maddie found Luke staring from where he'd finished loading fresh bread into baskets and placing them on the white shelves behind them. Shelves that Ethan built. The teenager was a little white around his mouth.

"Sorry. You probably don't want to hear more about my family drama."

Luke ran a hand through his short fair hair. "Family dramas aren't new to me. You were there for me when mine were being a nightmare. I'd like to help you with yours if I can."

Luke's father was a hard man, and Luke had not been his favorite child, which he'd made very clear more than once. Thankfully, they seemed to have made amends in their relationship, and it was touching that he would offer to help, but she shook her head.

"There's nothing anyone can do right now. It's a waiting game."

"As usual." Angel rolled her eyes.

"Mom's been tight-lipped about the whole thing. I get the impression her fear is mainly for her husband and that she's the one potentially putting him in danger. He should be arriving in Destiny today. Maybe he'll come to find her?" Maddie tapped her thigh.

"Perhaps if we knew what William looked like we could keep an eye out for him," Angel said.

"That's a great idea. I wonder if Mom has a picture of him?" Maddie suddenly realized that she knew nothing about the man apart from the fact her mother seemed devoted to him. That unsettled her as much as the case.

Angel somehow tapped into Maddie's thoughts, as she so often did. "I still can't get used to the idea that your mom's married after all this time."

"It's a struggle to get my head around it too," Maddie agreed. "She never had a good word to say about marriage. A free spirit, was the way she described herself."

Angel touched a manicured red nail to her cheek. "I wonder what he's like."

Surprised again, Maddie almost laughed. "Mom hasn't said too much about William apart from how close he is to his brother. It's kind of odd, since Ava believes Nicholas is the one who poisoned her husband. Although, Ava also thinks he's after her."

"This Nicholas sounds awful!"

Maddie nodded. "I know. Anyway, Ethan's looking into him."

"Good." Angel eyed her carefully. "Does it bother you that you didn't know?"

After years worrying and yearning for her mom, Maddie didn't want to be resentful about any of this. "Only a little. I can't picture myself as a flower girl or a bridesmaid, but it would have been nice to know before this. Mom's been kind of predictable up until now, and a husband doesn't fit into how Gran and I have grown accustomed to thinking of Ava."

Angel smiled gently. "Perhaps there's more to her

marriage than she's telling us. Or it could actually be true love?"

Her friend knew Ava as much as Maddie did, which was to say as much as her mom would allow anyone to know her. Until William.

Maddie grimaced. "I'm prepared to rule it out without more evidence."

Angel snorted, instantly putting her hand to her mouth. "Sorry. It's just that you're beginning to sound like Ethan more each day."

Maddie decided to take it as a compliment. "Thanks. I know he'd tell me that not all evidence should be believed. Mom's acting as if she thinks a lot of William, but who knows?"

"Here we go again. You may be looking for more trouble than there is."

Maddie stared at her friend. "You don't think poisoning is bad enough?"

"There's no confirmation yet, is there?"

"And that's why you're my best friend. You've always been able to corral my enthusiasm for getting to the bottom of things." Maddie grinned.

"Let's not get carried away. I try, is all." Angel took a quick look at the door and lowered her voice. "So, is the party on or off?"

"I want to say it's on, but I thought Mom would go this morning. I can't see how we can go ahead with this hanging over us, but let me talk to Ethan before we decide."

Angel nodded. "By the way, did you transfer last night's cooking class to tonight?"

Maddie grimaced, having completely forgotten about it. "Yes. I can't put them off again, as there's only a couple more weeks for this round. After that I'll have a short break before starting the next one. Now that the bakery is open on Saturdays, the week is pretty hectic."

Angel tutted the way Gran did when they were worried about her.

"You're a workaholic these days, and I think it's about time the four of us did something together. Also, I'd like to take some more lessons, perhaps in that next group. I've been very slack with using any of my previously gained knowledge, and I fear I may have forgotten everything you taught us."

Maddie shook her head. "There's no need to wait. You know you're welcome in the class anytime."

"Thanks, sugar. I missed a few of the classes through one thing or another, so I didn't think it fair to start now. It would be awful to hold the others back."

"I wish you'd told me that's how you felt. Come tonight; there's space, and I promise the recipe will be yummy and not too difficult."

"Says the expert. Okay, I'll come," Angel said eagerly.

Maddie wasn't sure if Angel was coming more to chat or bake but it didn't matter. When she was teaching, Maddie was in another of her happy places. This was fortuitous, since with her mom in town she needed plenty of those and also an outlet for her thoughts.

The bell tinkled over the front door.

Laura was back from the bank. "Hey, Angel. After more doughnuts?" she teased.

Angel grinned. "You know it. Hey, we've been talking about doing something as a group. What do you think?"

Laura reached behind the counter and grabbed her apron. "I have no ideas, but whatever it is, count me in."

"Really? I thought you'd be busy walking Deputy Jacob's dogs?" Angel teased right back.

Laura's cheeks colored. "I like to walk. He walks his dogs. Sometimes we meet up and walk together. End of story."

"Aha. Well I'll see you tonight, Maddie, and we'll talk soon about the other things." Angel winked at them and walked out the front to her shop two doors along from the bakery.

"What things?" Laura asked nervously.

"Just our get-together and the party." Maddie's voice dropped when a group from the community center came in.

They said they were there for coffee and cupcakes. What they wanted was information about Ava.

Chapter Six

For the whole day, gossip was rife in the bakery. Usually Maddie could turn the other cheek, but when it concerned her mom that was impossible. She couldn't lie about her mom being here, because Bernie had already told a couple of people before Gran could warn him. That was all it took.

As soon as the shop was closed, Maddie headed across the road from the bakery for a much-needed breath of fresh air and change of scenery. The park encompassed a corner site with a wood at the far end. To the left it circled in behind more shops, and to the right it headed down Plum Place, abutting Gran's front paddocks.

Right now Gran had no animals other than chickens, so a neighboring farmer used them for his own cattle. They were used to Maddie and paid her no mind as she walked by the fence.

Big Red ran ahead, scampering amongst the early spring flowers, chasing a butterfly. It was a peaceful walk on a good day and no doubt better enjoyed when one didn't have so much to think about. Between her mom and the party, Maddie couldn't pick which was the easiest to deal with.

Intending to walk around the perimeter a few times, when they got to the edge of the wood it appeared her companion had other ideas. Maddie called to him, but with a quick glance her way, he continued on the mission that was clearly more important than heeding her. With a sigh at recalcitrant pets, she reluctantly followed him into a thicket.

She heard him and moved faster. Something wasn't right. When she finally found him, Big Red was sitting on a log facing away from her, his ears flicking at speed. Turning only his head, he called her in a pitiful way and refused to budge from his perch when she called again.

Unable to believe he could have hurt himself in a place he frequented, she nevertheless pushed worriedly through the last brambles. She hadn't quite reached him when her heart seemed to miss a beat. There, under the log, half covered in weeds and what looked like strategically placed branches, was a hand. Clawed, one finger pointed at her.

"Hello?" she called hopefully, even as her stomach clenched and her heart raced.

Maddie knelt beside the hand, not ready to investigate the condition of the rest of the body, which was still hidden. With a large breath in, she placed two fingers on the cold wrist to feel for a pulse. Her breath hissed out. *Definitely deceased.*

Big Red jumped from the log and sniffed at the hand while Maddie pulled out her phone with a shaky hand.

Ethan answered on the first ring. "Hey. I was just thinking about you."

Ordinarily that would have delighted her, but that finger made her uneasy. Not that a dead body wouldn't have the same effect, but this was truly horrible. She glanced around the area, not sure what she thought was out there.

"Maddie?" Ethan brought her back to the call.

The words came out in a rush. "It's not good news, I'm afraid. Can you come to the park? Big Red's found a body."

Ethan's answer was a groan tempered with disbelief. "You checked?"

Despite being alone, Maddie nodded. "Yep. No pulse."

His voice softened. "Are you okay, sweetheart?"

"I have Big Red, but can you hurry?" She grimaced at the hand.

"I'll be there soon. I promise."

Feeling better when she heard his chair scrape and knowing he was on his way before he hung up, Maddie still couldn't help scanning the woods for anything or anyone. She called Big Red again, and to her relief he followed her to another log a few feet away. This felt a better place to wait for Ethan.

Suddenly cold, she pulled the ginger moggy to her chest.

"I wonder who he is?"

Big Red mewled in answer, wriggling to get down. Obviously he wanted to check out the curiosity in the grass a little more now he knew she was okay, but Maddie held him firmly.

"Stay with me. Ethan will want us to steer clear of the site so we don't contaminate it."

He nuzzled her chin as if to say he wouldn't dream of disturbing anything, and she slipped a finger under his collar, not allowing him the chance.

If she'd learned anything from their forays into cases with the sheriff, it was to not damage any evidence. Maybe "learned" was a strong word, but she was getting better at being careful. Which unfortunately meant that she'd had several opportunities to get it right.

Sitting as still as her cat would allow, it seemed a very long time before she heard a sound to her right. Her watch showed it had only been fifteen minutes.

"We're over here!" she called.

Ethan immediately appeared between the trees, and Big Red wriggled with more fervor. He wanted to say hi to Ethan, and while Maddie was delighted that her two men were so close, she was sure that the sheriff would be focused on the body before a friendly cat.

Ethan smiled gently from across the small glade, and despite the gruesome reason for them being in the secluded area, her heart danced a fast salsa the closer he got. She stood, holding on to her heavy handful, expecting a kiss hello. But right behind Ethan came Deputy Jacobs wearing a mischievous expression. She simply gave them a weak smile, hoping to hide her disappointment, then pointed toward the body.

"Over there. Like I said, he's definitely dead."

"Any idea who it is?" Ethan asked, scoping out the area as he moved carefully forward.

Maddie shook her head. "I didn't look any closer than his hand, and that was only to check for a pulse."

"Then how do you know it's a man?" Deputy Jacobs rubbed Big Red between the ears and tried not to grin when the cat nudged him for more.

"Look at the size of that hand. Unless it's a female weightlifter, I'm picking it's a male," Maddie told him, tamping down a measure of pride that she'd noticed this small detail.

Ethan leaned down to the hand and with a pencil moved some of the vegetation behind for a better look at the body it was attached to. "You're right. It's a man. Late thirties—maybe early forties. He hasn't been here too long by the looks of it. The broken branches are still green. I wonder what he's pointing at."

The three of them followed the direction of the finger, but it was toward a boulder and more brambles. A siren sounded in the distance.

"That was fast. The paramedics were out on a call when I rang, so I assumed they'd be a while," Deputy Jacobs told them.

Maddie shrugged. "It's Monday. The crew generally take people who can't get there under their own steam for their doctors checkups and hospital visits. I guess they thought this is more important."

"Mmmm."

Ethan was back to studying the body, which Maddie still wasn't able to see, no matter how much she craned her neck. With the men here it felt okay to be curious. Besides, this wasn't their first time in a similar situation. She blanched at the thought of this becoming a habit.

"Was he killed here?" she asked.

"We don't know he was killed," Deputy Jacobs said over his shoulder, then to Ethan, "I'll go show them where to come."

Maddie put Big Red on the ground but held on to his collar. "Surely, to be buried beneath carefully placed greenery indicates he didn't put himself there?"

Ethan snorted. "You're getting a little too good at this."

Maddie wasn't offended. With the cases she'd been involved in over the last year, she'd found out a great deal about murder, which admittedly sounded weird in her head.

Her grandad had passed down a heavy dose of curiosity

and that wasn't all. Busy with the secret service until he retired, he'd taken time to teach her self-defense and to guard against jumping to conclusions, because things were often not as they seemed. Gran had seemed oblivious to most of his training, but lately it appeared she'd simply turned a blind eye to all but the ones she found most troubling.

Shooting rabbits was necessary on a farm, and Maddie was a crack shot. She could also get herself out of most knots and handle a knife. These were things she didn't brag about, and when finding herself knee-deep in a case, she'd employed several tactics to keep herself and those she loved alive. It also appeared that Ava was fully aware of the extent of his teachings.

Ethan pulled out gloves from one of the many pockets of his uniform and slipped them on. From another he extracted a small camera and proceeded to take pictures from different angles, moving branches to do so.

"What were you doing here? It's a little off the track for your walks."

Maddie watched everything he did with interest. "Big Red led me to the body. I don't know how he knew about it."

"Animals can smell things and sense things we can't."

"And he's particularly clever." Maddie nuzzled the ginger fur.

Ethan crouched lower. "Ah."

"What is it?" She craned her neck this way and that, trying to see around him, but she was too far away.

"The back of his head has a massive gash. Although, there's not a great deal of blood here." Ethan sounded puzzled.

"Which indicates the murder happened somewhere

else and the body was dumped here at a later time," she stated.

When Ethan wasn't totally quiet, he tended to talk to himself, which gave Maddie the opportunity to pump him for information he'd be more guarded about when others were around.

"Yep" was his offering as he checked pockets.

"Any ID?"

"Nothing."

Maddie glanced around her. "I wonder where the murder weapon is. The killer would hardly bring it with the body, would he?"

"Hardly." Ethan stood, frowning as he scoped the area, picking up a couple of rocks and replacing them carefully. "There's nothing here, but it could have been dropped somewhere further away. Or the incident didn't happen here at all. Anyway, here's the paramedic."

Maddie knew that look. Ethan had said as much as he cared to. He had a lot to think about, and she didn't want to distract him. But before she went, she wanted to see the dead man's face, which would be covered as soon as Ethan gave the word to the paramedic.

Climbing on the log, she let go of Big Red, who bounded over to Ethan and rubbed against his leg. Guiltily, Maddie managed a quick look while Ethan was detained. The man was dark-haired—cut short, twigs stuck to it. He wore jeans and a dark sweater that looked well made. That was all she got before Ethan's raised eyebrow meant she was out of time.

"I'll see you later?" she asked hopefully.

"I wouldn't count on it, but I'll try." He offered a small smile before greeting the paramedic who was carrying a board for the body.

Maddie nodded at the man, who shook his head at her in wonder. She guessed her presence was getting to be a regular occurrence at this kind of thing, and that made things a little awkward.

Calling Big Red, she made a wide berth of the area. Deciding she wasn't capable of focusing on the cooking class scheduled for tonight, she would ring her students and postpone until tomorrow. If she could, she would have moved it to next week for a double class, except that was the week of Gran's birthday. There was slim chance of it going ahead, but if it did she'd have too much to do.

With the body being moved and no one paying him any attention, Big Red was happy to leave with Maddie. They walked swiftly back to the bakery, and Maddie rang her students straight away, careful to evade the exact reason for the postponement. Everyone was happy to come on Tuesday apart from Nora Beatty, who could be difficult at the best of times.

Maddie sighed with relief after her last call. Hopefully, by tomorrow things might be clearer about the dead man, and the town would rest easy again, because they would surely all know by morning.

Speaking of which, Ava and Gran had been together for a good part of the day, and Maddie thought that was probably long enough. She set off again with Big Red, who never liked to be omitted from an outing, especially ones to the cottage.

Chapter Seven

Ava sat on the edge of Grandad's recliner by the front door, looking ready to bolt when she saw Maddie coming up the path.

Maddie nodded, scraping her boots on the spikey hedgehog boot cleaner situated at the door. The grass had been damp at the park, and anyone with common sense would do likewise so as not to incur Gran's wrath by mucking up her floors or carpets.

"Hello, Madeline." Ava startled Maddie with the cool greeting and by following her into the utility room.

"Hello, Mom."

"Busy day?"

Well, this was awkward, but at least her mom was trying to converse. Only, Maddie was also out of practice. "Very."

"Where's the boyfriend? He seems as infatuated with you as he was when you were teenagers, and I assumed he'd be with you every minute of the day."

Maddie's skin prickled, undecided whether her mother was attempting conversation or being deliberately insulting.

"He's on an important case. I imagine he'll be involved with that for most of the evening."

"An important case? In Maple Falls?" Ava laughed shrilly.

"We get them, even here," Maddie replied stiffly.

"Nothing much happened when I lived here, although I did hear that you and the sheriff are involved in cases on a regular basis."

It almost sounded like a question, and Maddie had that premonition of dread she often associated with her mom. "I wouldn't say it was a regular occurrence."

"But you do spend a lot of time together? Any wedding bells in the air?"

"Mom!"

"What? A mother can't ask a simple question about the boyfriend's intentions?"

Gran was setting the table for dinner. "Stop teasing her, Ava. You gave up rights to know what Maddie is up to when you left her behind. She'll tell you when there's something to tell."

Ava threw herself onto a chair, almost overbalancing, and just missed Big Red with a flailing leg. Maddie wasn't sure if her mom was simply mad at Gran or embarrassed about her near miss but now she was red-faced and ornery.

"Can we just have one conversation without you bringing up the past?"

Gran nodded. "One day. When you're not bringing the past home with you."

Immediately Ava was contrite. "Look, I didn't mean to bring any trouble your way. Usually I can handle things for myself. This is different."

Gran added water glasses. "We know, and we forgive you, dear."

"Forgiven, but not forgotten?" Ava mused.

"That's about it. Why don't you tell us about your husband instead?" Gran took the seat next to Ava and nodded for Maddie to sit opposite them.

Ava gave them a nervous look, then sighed. "William is wonderful. He has many important acquaintances around the world, but he keeps a low profile because he's a quiet man and doesn't like too much fuss."

Hearing sincerity and affection in Ava's voice caught Maddie off guard. "Didn't it occur to you to invite Gran and me to the wedding?"

Ava's eyes widened. "What for? You'd have hated it. Both of you."

Gran tilted her head. "I don't know why you'd think that. We might have liked to decide for ourselves."

Ava snorted. "It was in Las Vegas."

"Oh." Gran grimaced at the idea.

"Exactly. Not really your thing, is it?"

"I'm sure it didn't have to be there. Especially if your husband is the quiet type," Gran insisted.

Ava shrugged. "It was a spur of the moment thing. William is busy, so we took the opportunity when he had to go there for business. That way we didn't have to invite his family either. They were certainly more upset than you two."

Her mom might be playing this down, but a frown marred her brow, and Maddie's curiosity overcame her shock. "Why would your marriage upset them?"

"Because of me. I'm nothing as far as his brother is concerned. White trash. They think the marriage was all my idea and that I coerced William into it."

Gran's breath whistled out and she slammed a hand on the table. "You are not white trash. *We* are not white trash."

Ava held up a hand. "Okay, so those words were not exactly spoken but I knew what Nicholas was thinking."

"We're hardly poor either," Gran added stiffly.

Ava snorted. "You can't possibly compare the two lifestyles."

"I don't know what you mean by that, but it makes no difference," Gran protested. "We have everything we need."

"Besides, what does it matter how much we have in the bank?" Maddie asked.

"It matters a great deal to Nicholas. He doesn't want William attached to someone who has no money and appears to be a gold digger. And now I can't reach him or Jerry." Ava bit back a sob and made a big deal about checking for something in her bag.

To give her mother a moment, Maddie looked out the dining room window to the large garden where Laura was weeding. A thought swirled around her head and settled heavily on her heart.

"How tall is William?"

Ava had always stated that she liked tall men—it was a deal breaker as far as she was concerned, but this was not the real reason Maddie asked. The John Doe at the park hadn't appeared to be very tall.

"About our height, or marginally taller. Maybe five eight." Ava's lips trembled.

Maddie couldn't help grimacing. "Would Nicholas ever hurt his brother?"

Ava's attention refocused, and her voice was harsh. "William wouldn't even think about the possibility. I have my suspicions, but why do you ask?"

Gran leaned forward and looked deep into Maddie's eyes. "You know something. Or something's happened."

Ethan wouldn't be happy with her telling anyone about

the body but Maddie could never lie to Gran. "I shouldn't say anything."

Ava also leaned toward Maddie. "Don't hold back on my account. I've seen a lot of ugly. More than you can imagine. Tell me what you know, especially if it concerns my husband."

The demanding tone should have put Maddie off, yet their whole relationship was dysfunctional, so when Gran nodded, and against her better judgement, the words slipped out. "A body's been found."

Blood drained from her mom's face. "William?"

Naturally, that's how it sounded and Maddie was annoyed with herself. "I'm not saying that, but do you have a photo of your husband?"

"To check in case it is him?" Ava demanded hoarsely.

"Actually, I'd like to see what my . . . stepfather looks like." The words were unnatural on Maddie's tongue as she willed her mom to calm down.

Ava twisted her hands several times before fetching her bag. A few seconds later, she placed a photo in front of Maddie. William looked nice. Dark hair. Round face. Clean shaven. Laughter lines around his eyes as he smiled at the camera.

Maddie shook her head in relief. "The man I found does look a little like him, but it isn't William."

Ava grabbed Maddie's forearm, fingers digging into her skin. "Are you positive it's not him?"

Seeing her mother so upset was a revelation and yet confusing. Ava wasn't pretending. She truly cared for her husband, which went against everything Maddie knew about her. She was a love 'em and leave 'em kind of woman. Or so she'd professed to be, and the town had agreed.

Maddie peeled off the fingers, reminded gruesomely of the one in the woods. "I am. What does Nicholas look like?"

Ava's eyes widened. "Similar to William. I mean, you can tell they are family but Nicholas is taller and thinner."

Maddie shook her head again. "I don't believe this man was tall, and he was quite stocky."

Ava's eyes widened. "This body—it looked like my husband, you say?"

"That's right. Why?"

"I've been trying to get hold of William's cousin. His phone keeps ringing but there's no answer." Ava paled again.

Maddie frowned. "What does his cousin have to do with this?"

Her mother resumed wringing her hands. "Marcus looks very much like William. Nearly as tall and stockier."

Maddie gasped. "You think he might be the person we found?"

Ava trembled. "I truly hope not, but it's possible. William asked him to bring me here, but I thought Marcus was now waiting in Destiny for William and Jerry."

"You should come down to the station. Ethan will want to talk to you." Maddie stood.

"The police station?" Ava trembled. "Do you think he was murdered?"

Maddie tapped her thigh. "I don't honestly know and it's probably too early to be certain. Will you come?"

Her mom frowned. "I suppose so. I just don't like those places."

"Our sheriff's station is nice and friendly," Maddie assured her, wondering how many times her mom had been through the doors of a police station.

Ava snorted, but stood and picked up her bag from a

chair. Grateful for the easy capitulation, Maddie jumped up from her seat.

Gran interrupted. "Maddie will need to collect her car. Unless you fancy the walk?"

Ava raised an eyebrow. "Are you kidding me? The station is not that close. I'll wait here."

Maddie didn't bother to answer. Kissing Gran, and with Big Red once more at her heels, she jogged back to the bakery. As soon as she got inside, she called Ethan while feeding Big Red. He was starving after his adventure, despite having persuaded Gran to give him a treat or two.

Then she thought about the dead man and that potentially a killer was in Maple Falls. Frustratingly, but not unusually, her call went to voicemail so Maddie locked up and headed out to the garage. Honey waited in her splendor. The old jeep was a high school graduation present from her grandad, who had lovingly taught her how to maintain the perfect condition she'd been in more than a decade earlier.

Maddie backed Honey out into Plum Place. Night was falling and shadows lengthened along the short drive. The huge maple trees all along the fence line of the paddocks stretched toward the middle of the narrow lane. A nervous person might think this ominous, but to Granddad's credit, Maddie didn't scare easily.

Outside the cottage, she honked the horn. Ava came outside and down the walk. She wore jeans and a light pink sweater. Her hair, wavy like Maddie's, was cut to shoulder length, and she looked great. Although, once she got in the car, Maddie could see dark circles around her eyes through the makeup.

Not knowing where William was or how he was doing

was obviously causing her mom some distress, and Maddie felt sorry for her.

"I see you haven't moved on in cars. I guess it fits the location, although I can't think why you left New York." Ava screwed up her face in distaste.

Almost immediately, her mom's attitude dissolved the tenderness Maddie felt. "Why would I move on from something that suits me perfectly and makes me happy?"

Ava made a rude noise, and Maddie let it be. Her mom had never been happy anywhere or with anyone so she couldn't appreciate the things that Maddie did. Except, she did seem genuinely upset about her husband. An awkward silence fell until they neared the station.

"So you love William?" Maddie gulped at her own outspokenness.

Ava frowned. "What kind of question is that?"

Maddie was curious about it from the moment she heard Ava had married, and now that she'd said the words, it seemed important to know. "A simple one, I thought."

Ava gave her a piercing look, and when Maddie didn't back down, she shrugged. "I married him, didn't I?"

Maddie wasn't buying her indifference. "Because you love him?"

"Obviously." Her mother moved as if the seat had suddenly grown tacks.

Was it obvious? Maddie didn't think so. He was clearly rich, so was that the main reason? They'd arrived at the station so she wasn't going to get more from her mom.

They got out and Maddie knocked on the front door. The lights still burned out the back when Deputy Jacobs came into the reception area from the hall. He was surprised to see them, and switched on more lights before quickly unlocking the door.

"Evening, ladies. What can I do for you?"

Rob had been aloof when Maddie first came back to town, but these days he was incredibly obliging, and he had a sweet fondness for Laura that Maddie hoped to encourage.

"Is Ethan around?" Maddie peered around him to the hall.

Rob shook his head. "He's gone to the hospital to meet Detective Jones."

"Is it about the body?"

Rob nodded, looking curiously at Ava and then back to Maddie.

She took a deep breath. "That's why we're here. My mom might know who it is."

Rob's eyebrows shot up his forehead like they were trying to escape into his hair. "Just a minute." He ran down the short hall, and Maddie heard him telling someone he was going to the hospital. Then he was back with his keys, a line of worry across his brow.

"You need to come with me," he said.

Ava took a step back. "Why? Where are you taking us?"

"To the hospital. With no fingerprint matches yet, they need you to identify the body."

Maddie had half expected this, but her mom, who maybe hadn't had the same experiences with the law, was pale and shaking slightly.

Not giving them more time to react, Rob led the way to a marked car out the back. Maddie followed with Ava dragging her heels behind them. Before they set off, Rob called Ethan and, when he too had no luck, tried Detective Jones. Successful, Rob gave him a quick rundown before pocketing his phone. "He'll meet us at the morgue."

This time Maddie did shiver, keeping her mom

company in the nervous stakes. Nothing truly prepared a person to see a dead body. The first time would naturally be worse, and Maddie wasn't immune to her mother's worry. She simply didn't know what to say.

They may look alike, but their take on life was vastly different, and small talk had never been something her mother took an interest in. Look at the avoidance of talking about love. Also, Maddie was scared of the answers if she asked more pertinent questions. So they stared out their respective windows for most of the drive into Destiny, where the closest hospital was.

When they neared it, Maddie turned. "Are you okay?"

Ava stiffened, hands clasped neatly on her lap. "I'm fine."

"Are you upset because you might know the man?" Maddie couldn't help asking.

"If it's him, then of course I'll be upset." Ava's voice shook. "He's William's best friend as well as his cousin and assistant. And a very sweet man."

She'd added the last sentence softly, and Maddie heard that she cared for Marcus. The issue Maddie had was that Ava had only known the two men for what amounted to a couple of months. Yet, somehow, her cold mom had formed deep relationships with both of them. It was baffling, and Maddie was at a loss as to how to comfort her mother.

There was no time to figure it out right now, since they were pulling up to the hospital. Deputy Jacobs drove around the back to wide doors. An ambulance sat close to it, engine off, with paramedics checking their equipment.

With Rob in the lead, they walked quickly through the large double doors and then on to the elevators at the end of the hall.

"Hold the door!"

Chapter Eight

etective Jones ran down the hall toward them. "Thank you." He nodded, slightly out of breath.

"Good evening, Detective. This is my mother, Ava Fl—" Maddie felt the heat rise in her cheeks. It might take a while to get used to the name change. "Ava Blackwell."

The detective wore his usual long black coat and sober expression, but she thought she detected a small twinkle in his eyes as he entered the elevator. A little shorter but much broader than Ethan, he was often a whole lot less friendly. She took a second look, but it was gone, so perhaps she had indeed imagined it.

"Let's talk when we get downstairs," he said without a glimmer of anything but professionalism.

Downstairs was surely where the maybe-cousin was, and they arrived at their floor far sooner than Maddie would have liked. The detective led them down several corridors, and somehow it felt darker and eerie, yet the lighting was probably no different to the floor they'd just come from. But it definitely felt cooler.

Their footsteps echoed around them, and Maddie's skin prickled. She'd seen more dead bodies than she cared to count, but she had to admit that not knowing the victim was a little easier on the nerves. Then she stumbled slightly as the thought occurred to her that this man was, in some twist of fate, potentially related to her. Even though they'd never even met, the thought did make her a little ill.

No one seemed to notice the effect this realization had on her, and a rush of relief hit when she saw a familiar figure at another doorway. Ethan gave her a quick, encouraging smile, and she responded in kind, not wanting him to be worried about her as well as the case.

He held the door for them. "Thanks for coming so quickly, Mrs. Blackwell. These days we usually have a photo instead of a physical viewing, but with no ID we weren't prepared for you coming forward so quickly."

Ava stared, feet dragging even more as she passed by him and saw the gurney in the middle of the sterile room. It was obvious that the crisp white sheet covered a body. Ava gulped, her eyes full of fear.

Ethan stood between her and the gurney. "I appreciate this isn't easy," he said gently. "We have counselors available if you need someone to talk to about this."

"That won't be necessary." Ava didn't meet his eyes.

Ethan moved out of her way. "Take your time and let me know when you're ready."

Standing in a semicircle, they waited patiently for Ava to signal her readiness. The detective signaled to a man dressed in a long white coat who waited solemnly to one side. The man picked up two corners of the fabric and pulled it down enough to reveal only the dead man's face.

Ava gasped, nodding once more as she took a step back.

Her distress was real, and Maddie felt her throat constrict. Despite at times yearning for any emotion other than frustration to come her way, she had never wished her mom sadness.

Attempting to hug Ava, she was rebuffed by a simple twist of her mom's body. It wasn't the first time Maddie felt the pain of her mom's rejection, but it hurt more in that moment than it had in a long time. Still, this wasn't about her, and Maddie took a deep breath to settle the inner turmoil. Grief did strange things to a person, and everyone handled it in their own way.

Detective Jones moved to the door. "I have a room down the hall where you can make a statement when you're ready, Mrs. Blackwell."

Ava didn't need to be asked twice, leaving the room as fast as she could and without a backward glance.

Maddie sighed as the sheet was replaced. Ethan touched her shoulder, and she looked up into those deep blue eyes, feeling the warmth of his love.

"I'm sorry this is happening to you," he said softly.

She sighed again. There was no need to explain to Ethan how she was feeling—he'd witnessed Ava's disinterest in Maddie for years. "I don't know why her attitude's affecting me so badly after all this time, but I can't make this about me right now."

"How can it not affect you? She's your mom and she's in trouble. Nothing Ava does or says can change that. Plus, you're a good person. Which is the easiest kind to hurt, in my humble opinion."

His wry grin made her smile, and he rewarded her with a quick kiss on the lips. "I have to go join the interview. How about we meet upstairs in the café afterwards? Your mom might need some quiet time after all this."

"I'd kill for a cup of tea." Maddie gasped at the words, which were highly inappropriate given where they were.

Ethan's lips curved at the ends. "You'd be surprised how many times that exact phrase comes up at this sort of thing. Or maybe not."

He always knew the right thing to say. "I guess I'm not invited to the interview?"

"You guess right." Ethan led her back to the elevator. "I hope we won't be too long."

"Me too." She gave him a small wave as the doors closed. It was good to be out of the atmosphere of the morgue, and she'd feel better once she got home, but being with Ethan was a pretty good tonic too.

The café was still open, and she ordered tea and took a seat by a window. Seeing outside, even though it was dark, helped calm her. The tea was hot and strong, and Maddie inhaled the steam, which warmed her chilled hands and face.

According to Gran, tea was the remedy for most moods and malaise, and Maddie was inclined to agree. Ethan liked to tease her about this, but he had been known to have the odd cuppa when Gran was around.

Thinking of her reminded Maddie to call and give Gran an update. Not that there was much to report other than the dead man was in fact William's cousin, but Gran was thankful and made Maddie promise to take care of Ava.

Just how could she do that when her mom was so hard to help? How very ironic that Ava came home to find that very thing.

Determined not to go down that rabbit hole, Maddie pulled out the pad she always carried to work on recipes she might try or amend in the future. Angel was a doughnut addict, and Maddie was trying to find alternatives to tempt her. When she made something new or at least new to her bakery, she would take a sample down to the community center and let Gran's group try them, but Angel would always get the first taste.

Who wouldn't love the way they enjoyed her treats? There was never a bad review, apart from Nora Beatty, who found pleasure in being contrary.

With a slight smile, Maddie scribbled notes and quantities. After several minutes she stopped to tap the pen on her thigh. An idea that would work jumped out at her. This would be a new recipe for the cooking group and her interns, but not too difficult and would be fun for everyone.

She was so engrossed in her thoughts that a deep voice startled her.

"Eclairs? I love them."

Maddie jumped out of her seat to find a man standing beside her. "Pardon?"

He merely smiled. "Sorry to make you start. Unless I'm very much mistaken, you're Madeline."

Maddie gaped for a moment or two. His English accent, so much stronger than Gran's, was very proper. Well-dressed in a charcoal suit and open-necked white shirt, he definitely looked the part of a wealthy land owner.

"You're William Blackwell?"

He nodded. "I am. Your photo doesn't do you justice, but you are a replica of your mother, so I'd know you anywhere. At last we meet."

Maddie was stunned once more. Her mom had photos? That she actually showed people? Her inability to converse properly didn't appear to bother him.

"I didn't mean to intrude. The deputy told me to wait in here. Although, I'm not entirely sure why. He said that your mother was just fine and she would join me soon. You'd tell me if Ava wasn't well?"

He looked disturbed at the idea, and Maddie nodded, finally managing to speak. "Where did you come from?"

He winked. "England."

If she hadn't known that fact, his accent made it undeniable, but his resemblance to his cousin was indeed startling. What she couldn't accept was how odd it was that he deemed it okay to have a joke with her.

"I meant where did you come from today?"

At her tense tone, his eyebrows rose.

"I was just outside Destiny, waiting for a call from my cousin. Instead my lovely wife texted me to say to meet her here tonight. She said she was okay and wouldn't elaborate, but it does seem an odd place to meet. Wait, I can see you're upset. Something's wrong. Where's Ava?" He frowned and looked back to the sliding doors, where Deputy Jacobs was visible through the glass.

Horrified that the man had no idea about his cousin, Maddie held out a chair. "Please take a seat, Mr. Blackwell."

"You must call me William."

Ethan was a gentleman, but Mr. Blackwell was the English kind. Formal yet friendly—who else could carry that off? He certainly was nothing like Maddie could have envisaged her mom ending up with.

Suddenly, he reached out a large, rough hand to hold hers. "Please tell me Ava's okay."

She wasn't sure if Ethan wanted all the details told, but the earnestness on Mr. Blackwell's face touched Maddie, making sharing the news a necessity. Deputy Jacobs, visible over the man's shoulder, raised an eyebrow as if checking she was okay. She nodded. William didn't appear to be a threat, but she took a deep breath anyway. This wasn't going to be easy but the longer she took to tell him wouldn't change the facts. His cousin was deceased, and they couldn't sit here making small talk until Ava showed, with Maddie pretending everything was peachy.

"Mom's fine. Unfortunately, there is bad news."

He raised a thick black brow. "That's obvious, dear. It's not your gran?"

Maddie flinched at the endearment, but appreciated that the man was upset. Or maybe that was his manner. She took another deep breath. "Gran is just fine. I'm afraid that your cousin is dead."

He reared back. "Marcus? How? When?"

No one could possibly feign this level of disbelief and horror. Maddie squeezed his forearm. "Earlier today a body was found. Ava recognized the man's description and was brought to the hospital to identify him. I guess she didn't know you were close by."

William put his face in his hands for a moment, and his eyes were damp when he took them away. "She knew I would be arriving today, but not exactly when or where. Ava was so worried for my safety, she made me promise not to tell anyone. My phone stopped working, and Marcus went to purchase a new one. Then we were coming to collect Ava. With the length of time he'd been gone, I suspected something was wrong, but never dreamed. . . ." His words rushed out in an agonized way, and he finished on a small sob.

"I am so terribly sorry to give you this news." Maddie was at a loss how to console her mom's husband and looked to the door, hopeful that her mom would appear.

"I imagine someone had to. Poor Marcus." William gave a shuddering sigh, his fingers digging into the bridge of his nose. "This is all such a mess. I don't know why it's happening, and I'm so useless at figuring this out."

"Mom told me everything about the poisoning. I'm sorry you've been ill and that someone you know must have done it."

He sighed again. "It's understandable that Ava would need to confide in you. You're very important to her."

Maddie couldn't think of an answer that wouldn't sound sarcastic.

"Ava thinks I drank the poison intended for her, so I sent her away in case she was right." His eyes widened. "Perhaps Marcus was really the target?"

Maddie hadn't thought of that, but she had to ask, "Surely Maple Falls would be the first place anyone would look?"

William's cheeks flushed. "Ava said she would be safer with people she knew and that no one would guess she came from such a small town. I'm such a fool."

Maddie patted his hand. "I'm sure Mom was persuasive."

He almost smiled. "I didn't want to be separated, but Marcus also thought it wise. We're supposed to leave next week for England, and I hoped whoever was involved wouldn't find out about the flight details. Since Ava hired a bodyguard, someone she knew from the bar she'd worked at, I sent Marcus to keep an eye on her and report back to me." He suddenly rubbed his eyes. "I can't believe this. Marcus was far more than my assistant or cousin. Now he's gone because of me."

Maddie put her hand on his shoulder. "You can't blame yourself for someone killing Marcus. Did he find out anything prior to his death about the poisoning?"

William shook his head sadly. "Before he came here,

and after the police had done so, he spoke to my staff. He said he was happy that they were innocent." William grimaced. "I called him this morning, and he had no more clues or ideas who would try to poison me. There is a short list of people who had access to the sitting room and our food and drink, but the police told me before I snuck out of the hospital that the case is still very much wide open."

"So no one knew that you were coming here either?"

"No. I listened to Marcus and Ava and kept it to myself and my bodyguard." His eyes were misty. "I owe your mother my life. She was in the suite when I began to choke on nothing and called the ambulance straight away. The hospital recognized the almond-like smell and got the poison out of my system pretty quickly."

"She loves you." The words came out just fine, but it was still a shock to hear them from her own mouth, and even more of a shock that Maddie believed them to be true.

His quivering smile was followed by an endearing earnestness. "And I love her. She's brought so much to my staid life in a short time. I would do anything to keep her safe."

Maddie searched his face. "It seems as though you are both in danger."

He shrugged. "I'm not so sure. The cocktail was on the table, and I assumed it was for me, but according to Ava, she'd ordered it for herself."

"Did the police find the poison that was used?"

"Nothing was found to point to where it came from. Marcus brought the drink to the room without knowing who made it. You can imagine how upset he was."

He sounded so anguished that Maddie made the soothing sound that Gran was well known for and changed the subject.

"Mom never said where you and she lived after the wedding."

He wiped his face with a white handkerchief he pulled from his jacket pocket. "I leased a penthouse suite in Hollywood soon after we met. I was stupidly trying to impress your mom. Do you know that the only reason we got together was that she felt sorry for me?"

Maddie was surprised. "What on earth for?"

"She was serving me at a bar and being spoken to roughly. I intervened and got a thump to the chin for my troubles." He rubbed his chin as though he could still feel it.

"She's the prettiest woman I've ever seen, and so feisty. She gave that patron a tongue lashing on my behalf, and I was smitten. Unfortunately, she got fired and was pretty mad with everyone, including me." Even in his sadness, the memory made him smile.

Maddie felt her cheeks heat. She knew little about her mom's life, so this was a lot to take in, but the anger at everyone around her was only too real.

"I insisted she come work for me, and maybe she felt as though she had no choice at the time, but it worked out perfectly," he continued.

This conversation was full of surprises. If her mom hadn't wanted to be employed by William, she would have said no without a qualm. "What sort of work?"

"Mostly correspondence."

Maddie couldn't imagine her mom sitting at a desk. "I'm sure that a break from bar work would be nice. Were there a lot of people around your penthouse when it happened?"

"Not really. There were the hotel staff who'd cleaned earlier, Marcus, and Nicholas had a suite next to ours. As I said, your mother and I were supposed to be leaving for England next week, and my secretary had already returned home." He hesitated for a moment. "If only we'd left as well."

Her mom's departure was news to Maddie, and she felt another wave of disappointment at the secrecy of Ava's life. "Back to the castle you've inherited?"

William nodded. "That's right. Ava told you about Craigavon Castle?"

"She mentioned it, but not its name. How did you inherit it?"

Before he could answer, a commotion sounded outside the room. Maddie saw Rob dart outside.

The doors opened, but the entrance looked empty.

Chapter Nine

The lift pinged its arrival, and the doors slid open to reveal Ava and Ethan. William stood and swiftly crossed the room toward his wife, who ran into his open arms. She began to cry softly into his shoulder as he kissed the top of her head. They were similar in height, her blonde head fitting naturally into the side of his neck.

Maddie felt a lump in her throat. No matter their differences, she'd always hoped that one day her mom would find happiness. It looked like she truly had, and Maddie was glad.

Ethan coughed. "Mr. Blackwell, I'm Sheriff Tanner."

Rob must have conveyed the message that the victim's cousin had arrived. Mr. Blackwell leaned forward, keeping one arm around Ava, and held out his hand.

"Madeline has told me the news about my cousin. May I see Marcus?"

If Ethan was bothered by Maddie preempting him, he didn't show it.

"I'll take you there now. Afterwards we'd like to ask you some questions."

While speaking gently, Ethan gave the impression that he expected nothing but compliance.

Ava clutched her husband's arm, her face full of concern. "Do you need me to come with you?"

William patted her hand. "I'm sure once was enough, dear. You wait here with your lovely daughter."

"Are you sure?"

With a lingering kiss on her forehead, William smiled softly. "It will be fine, my love. I'll be back soon."

Ethan glanced around the room. "Where's Deputy Jacobs?"

Maddie slapped her forehead. "He ran outside a while ago."

Ethan looked worried, but just then Rob came through the doors, frog-marching a tall fair-haired man. His arms behind him, he wriggled and jerked trying to get free. When he turned, Maddie could see the cuffs.

William gasped. "Jerry!"

"You know him?" the deputy asked.

"This is my bodyguard, Jerry Sims. He's no threat," William protested.

Rob frowned. "I found him lurking by the door, then he suddenly ran off."

"And I told you who I was and that I was only doing my job. There's someone outside I was watching and I chased her."

Ethan stepped forward. "Who would that be?"

Jerry shrugged. "I don't know. Ever since we arrived today, she's been tailing us."

"She?" Rob scoffed.

"That's right." Jerry sounded defensive. "All I can say is that she's darn fast."

"You didn't see anyone else?" Ethan asked his deputy.

Rob shook his head, not seeming at all convinced of the man's innocence. "Shall I take him to the station?"

"But he can't be involved," Ava intervened. "We hired him after the poisoning."

Ethan made an abrupt decision. "Uncuff him, but he can come with Mr. Blackwell downstairs. Detective Jones will also want to talk to him."

Ava watched sadly as the men walked away. Her mom appeared so bereft and confused that Maddie put her arms around her. This time, and for the first she could remember, Ava allowed it.

"He seems very nice," Maddie said into her hair. The smell of her mom's fragrance brought back sketchy memories of when she was small. There was a time when she was held, she was sure of it.

"Nice? He's more than that. He knows all about my past and doesn't give a fig about it." There was a smattering of scorn, but then she added in a softer tone, "I know we've been together a short while, but William wants me to be happy and does all he can to make that happen. I finally feel like I belong somewhere. Thank you for taking care of him."

It was a shame that Ava couldn't also find happiness with the family she had, but Maddie sucked down a bout of self-pity. Along with Gran and Ethan, she would do everything in her power to keep her mom safe, regardless of Ava's attitude toward them.

Which meant they had to know everything, because there was an obvious missing piece to this puzzle. The killer had to have a motive, which implied it was someone they knew. William might be a savvy business owner, but he'd made a pretty awful mistake in agreeing where he and Ava would be safe. Maybe he was mistaken about who his friends were.

"Mom? Is there a reason someone might want to kill Marcus, other than being related to William?"

Her mother pulled away as if Maddie was on fire and likely to burn them both. "It's complicated."

"It always is." Maddie regretted her tone immediately but it was too late.

"I knew you would find a way to bring up the past. You and your gran can't think of me in any way other than as the bratty woman who left her child to be raised by someone else. My mother only ever saw the bad in me."

Maddie's anger bubbled inside her. She could take an awful lot of criticism from her mom, but to talk bad about Gran crossed the line.

"Until you arrived yesterday, we had no idea your life had changed. After a whirlwind romance of—I don't even know how long, you're married and on the run from a murderer! You can't expect our opinions to have a makeover in twenty-four hours. What I do know for a fact is that Gran and I have never stopped loving you and we've always been here waiting for you to come home. Even knowing we weren't important to you."

Ava gasped, and Maddie was shocked herself. Never in her life had she talked back to her mom. To be honest, it was quite liberating, even while she waited for the backlash.

Instead, Ava crumpled. Literally. She slipped into the chair her husband had so recently vacated, giving the impression that she'd be on the floor in a heap if the chair hadn't been available.

Maddie knelt beside her. "I'm sorry, Mom. It's not right for us to argue when you've lost someone you care about."

Ava put a hand up to ward off the embrace she could see was forthcoming. Maddie moved back a little, unprepared for her mother's next words or the tear that was brutally wiped away.

"As far as I'm concerned, it's never a good time to delve into the past, but I want to tell you that you have nothing to be sorry for. I left you. That's the truth. I knew it was wrong, and yet if we are honest, it was right for all of us. I couldn't stay in Maple Falls with everyone treating me like a leper. Small towns don't easily forget teenage pregnancies."

An apology in any form was a rare thing from her mom, and it rocked more of the perceptions Maddie had about her.

"I'm sure it was hard." Maddie didn't bring up how hard it had been to be the child in question. "Fortunately, times have changed and people are more accepting these days."

Ava snorted. "Maybe elsewhere, but not in Maple Falls. Each time I came back I was made to feel guilty every second. Guilty for loving a man who decided he didn't want me. Guilty that my parents had to face criticism over my actions. Guilty that you didn't have a father."

"I would have been happy just to have a mother." Maddie couldn't prevent the deep sadness that covered her words.

Ava shook her head. "A mother who wasn't me would be fine. I could never be the mother you should have. I knew your gran was. She did her best with me but I was a constant disappointment and so very angry. I needed to grow up and have the freedom to do so. To find out who I could be and not try to be what everyone expected."

Maddie gasped. "I never expected anything. Although, I did have a childish hope. But when you left the last time you made it terribly clear that you could never live here again. I accepted that. What I don't get is why you couldn't visit us—me—more often?"

Ava turned away, her face flushed. When a lengthy silence ensued, Maddie thought they were done. Then, her mom surprised her again.

"I did meet with your grandad several times. He'd tell me where you were, and I'd watch from a distance. You were very good at sport. A natural leader. You had plenty of close friends and you looked happy."

The blood pounded in Maddie's head. Father figure and her hero, Grandad had spoiled her and loved her unconditionally. Had he really lied to her for all those years?

"He never said a word. Why would he do that when he knew how I felt?"

"Because I swore him to secrecy. I couldn't handle seeing your face. Seeing the want in your eyes and knowing I couldn't come home. We'd all have been miserable."

Maddie stood. "You don't know that for sure."

Ava looked up and gave her a glimmer of a smile. "I do, and so do you."

Maddie walked over to the windows, when what she really wanted to do was run away from this room and her mom. Everyone had their own version of the truth and of the past. Hers held a memory of seeing her mom one particular Christmas.

Maddie had trailed after Ava, not speaking, simply watching every move. Hoping her mom would say she was home for good. Deep down she'd known it wasn't going to happen, but still she'd hoped. After all, it's what children did best, wasn't it? All that did was annoy Ava.

From the corner of her eye, Maddie could see Ava watching as she paced the room. For the first time Maddie didn't care if her mom noticed the fingers tapping her thighs. She'd developed this coping technique for anxiety, and people who knew her rarely commented, but her mom disapproved and had told her to stop many times. Today she didn't comment, and Maddie's hand slowed.

Her breath caught a little at the perceived betrayal. Her mom was Grandad's child, therefore she'd naturally take precedence in his loyalty. It hurt, but this was the only way Maddie could come to terms with it and not think badly of him.

"We'll have to agree to disagree about your absence. And I'm sure William would like to get out of here. If we're going to keep everyone safe, then you need to fill in the gaps with anything you can think of."

Ava crossed her arms. "I told you about the castle. It's all to do with that. Perhaps we should wait until the sheriff returns?"

Maddie nodded and went to the window again. It was dark outside and there were plenty of shadows. Who was this mysterious woman? And what part had she played in all of this?

Chapter Ten

They waited in an awkward silence for what seemed a very long time. When Ethan and William returned, relief washed over Maddie. William appeared shaken, and Ava hurried to his side. He wrapped her into his arms, and they stood motionless for a moment.

Ethan coughed. "We'll wait here until the detective has finished with your bodyguard," he told them.

"Meanwhile, Mom and William should explain about the castle he's inherited," Maddie suggested.

Ethan gave her a questioning look before directing it to the couple who were sitting close at the table. "Any information you have will be good."

When Ava finished, Ethan frowned. "So you believe that your brother-in-law wants to get his hands on the castle by getting rid of you. Assuming he's capable of such a thing, how would killing you allow that to happen?"

William looked ill, and his mouth opened as if he would refute the suggestion.

Ava noticed, paled, but continued. "If it was Nicholas, he'd have to kill William and me."

"But you said there was only one poisoned cocktail and you ordered it," Maddie noted.

"That's right." Ava nodded.

"If there were only the two of you and Nicholas there at the time, why don't you suspect your brother?" Ethan asked William.

"Family means a lot to us. We've had our share of losses, and I can't entertain the idea that my brother's capable of attempted murder, let alone murder. Plus, there's no proof." He sounded almost apologetic in his defense of his brother.

Frustration bristled from Ava.

"Yet, you're convinced it's him?" Ethan pressed.

Ava avoided William's hurt expression. "I can't help it. He looks at me with such distaste behind William's back. Whenever we're alone he says dreadful things about my past and my character. Marcus overheard him once and he asked Nicholas to apologize. When he refused, Marcus apologized on behalf of his cousin. He was so sweet." She gave a small hiccup.

"Didn't Marcus tell William what Nicholas said?" Maddie pressed.

"I'd hoped he would, but Marcus hated to cause trouble, and I didn't want him to be stuck in the middle of a family fight over me. He was loyal to both brothers and would do anything for them. That's why his death is so shocking."

Marcus had obviously made a huge impact on her mom if she wouldn't ask him to intervene with William against Nicholas.

Ava stole a look at William. Loving his family and now his wife so much, her husband was clearly torn about what or who to believe. That had to have an effect on Ava over and above Marcus's death, because William could only defend Nicholas at Ava's expense. Maddie shuddered.

Everyone else seemed depressed while Ethan made notes. The café had closed, but there was a machine on the far wall. Feeling drained, Maddie made them all coffee.

"It would be good if you could stay at the cottage until we get this sorted. We can get your things from your hotel tomorrow," Ethan said.

William frowned. "Wouldn't it be better for everyone if I'm elsewhere?"

Maddie shook her head. "That's not a good idea, Mr. Blackwell. Since we don't know who the target was, you need to have someone watching out for both of you."

"I'd really like you to call me William. After all, we are family. As for someone looking out for us, the last person who did that is lying on a cold tray downstairs." He pinched the bridge of his nose.

Maddie gulped. Mr. Blackwell . . . William, was hurting bad, no matter how staunch he might wish to appear. Yet, through his pain, he had included her as part of his family. She wasn't sure how to feel about that. More family was a good thing—if they were all as nice as William. That didn't appear to be the case.

Ethan stepped in to fill the silence. "We have no idea who killed Marcus or who could still be in danger. So you need to let us do our job."

He paused, perhaps to let them assimilate this. It appeared that Ava and her husband wished to protect each other more than themselves. Yet one more telling sign that her mom was indeed very much in love with her husband.

A sharp pain in her chest made Maddie realize that despite being happy for her mom, along with it came a sense of betrayal that she would never be loved in that way by Ava.

"Deputy Jacobs and I will keep an eye on the cottage through the night, then we can regroup tomorrow and decide on a better course of action."

Maddie gasped as an idea hit her. "But the body was found not that far from Gran's. Surely that indicates the murderer knows where Mom is staying?"

"Perhaps, but William's whereabouts will no doubt be known by now too. It will be best to have everyone together than try to watch several places." Ethan said this with patience and something more. Maddie could see he was trying to hide the depth of his worry, and that fueled her fear for everyone at the cottage, including Laura. She needed to get back there and help protect them in any way she could.

Having police outside or nearby wasn't the same as being inside, as she well knew. Which made her worry about who was protecting Gran and Laura right now. "If that's okay with Mom and . . . William, we should get to the cottage right away. I don't want Gran to worry."

Ava and William looked at each other.

"I guess we have no choice," Ava said in a heavy voice.

"Let me tell Rob what's happening. If everything checks out, he can bring the bodyguard with him." Ethan said.

When he was done, William took Ava's arm, and they filed out of the café, flanked by Maddie and Ethan. He led them to his car, and Maddie got in the passenger side.

The tension in the confined space was palpable, and again it was a quiet ride.

Chapter Eleven

L
ikely hearing the cars and seeing their lights, Gran opened the door in her dressing gown as soon as they arrived. Laura, similarly attired, stood behind her, peering out into the night.

Gran hugged Maddie and offered Ava a small smile, but her eyes sought out Ava's husband, giving him a long look as if she could assess his character in a moment or two.

"This is William Blackwell, Mom's husband." Maddie introduced him as they entered.

William took Gran's hand and kissed the back of it. "You must be Ava's mother. Her good looks obviously run in the family. I'm so pleased to meet you at last. I've heard a lot about you." He smiled, although his sadness could not be hidden.

Gran looked uncertainly to her daughter and then Maddie, who nodded encouragingly. A couple of days ago, Maddie would perhaps have not been so keen to have her mom's husband under their roof. Funny how things changed quickly.

A little flustered by all the late-night guests, especially

her new son-in-law, Gran nevertheless became the consummate host.

"I wish I could say the same, but perhaps we can change that over a nice cup of tea. Or would you prefer coffee?"

He smiled gratefully. "Tea would be wonderful."

"Please come in and make yourselves comfortable." Gran showed him the way.

"I'll leave you to the rest of your evening," Ethan said, already backing out the door. "Stay inside, and I'll be back in the morning." After his warning, he touched his hat to Gran and gave Maddie a searching look.

Knowing he had a lot to investigate and to oversee the stakeout, she'd still rather have him inside the cottage with everybody else. With her. She sucked down that slightly desperate thought and smiled, which fake or not seemed to give him a little relief.

A ginger dynamo launched himself at her ankles. Somehow Big Red had found her again. Happy to see her but annoyed at being left behind, he wound in and out of her legs, cuffing her heels as she went inside. Almost tripping several times, she couldn't be angry and picked him up to rub her face in his neck. A deep purr and a paw on her cheek meant she was forgiven. For now.

Standing in the dining room, Laura awkwardly tucked her dressing gown closer to her body, and Maddie introduced her to William.

He shook her hand, and Laura's flush was nearly as red as her hair. Any man's attention, no matter how innocuous, was a trial for her.

"Sorry to keep you all from your beds and to impose on you like this," William said.

Gran waved her hand. "Not at all. You're very welcome.

As I said, we can use the opportunity to get to know each other."

Ava rolled her eyes.

"I'll see if I can sleep at Angel's so you can have my room, Maddie," Laura said softly.

"It's late and too dangerous to be wandering down the road. Besides, I wouldn't dream of taking your room. If you could loan me a nightie, I'm happy to sleep on the chaise in the sitting room. Besides, I'm not ready to sleep just yet, and I'm sure we have a few things to discuss."

Maddie gave the rest of the group a searching look, convinced her mom wouldn't be as open as she'd been at the hospital. Regardless, Maddie wanted to chat more with William and thought he might be happy to do so if he wasn't all talked out by now.

Laura reluctantly agreed and disappeared upstairs. She returned quickly with a nightie that Gran would be equally comfortable in, since it would likely cover a body from head to toe. Maddie took it without comment, and her friend excused herself, bustling back upstairs.

Maddie got cups and saucers ready while Gran made tea, nodding Maddie toward the top shelf of the cabinet that housed other tea sets. The set Gran meant her to retrieve was one that rarely got used.

"William, would you mind getting this down for me," Maddie asked, since he was a little taller.

He obliged and handed it to her carefully. "These are wonderful. They remind me of spring at home."

Maddie agreed, but didn't explain the significance of them. Everyone who came to the cottage on a regular basis was given their own patterned set. Gran's had lilacs, Maddie's a delicate pink rose depicted on two sides and on its matching saucer. Angel—yellow daffodils. Suzy—white orchids with pink centers. Laura—a blue wisteria pattern. Ava—red sweet pea with tendrils wandering around the rim. Then there was the one William handed to Maddie.

No one commented as she gave the set a quick rinse. William looked confused, as though he sensed something significant taking place. Gran gave him a lovely smile and handed him the new set she'd recently acquired. It was royal blue with a white tulip gracing either side of the cup and the middle of the saucer. Somehow the patterns were always appropriate for the person.

Gran poured, and Maddie took a satisfied sip of the strong brew, wondering at the last twenty-four hours.

Ava held her cup between two hands, inhaling the fragrance. "No one makes tea quite like my mother," she said to her husband.

"It is good. Very similar to my own blend, which is wonderful since I never travel without it. Except for today. There wasn't time to go back to the apartment to get it," he said wistfully.

"I get my tea leaves sent over from England by my brother," Gran explained.

"Ah, yes. Ava's told me your heritage, and you still have an accent, which is nice." William was polite, even though his face was pinched.

Gran nodded. "I'm told by my friends that it's not as strong as it was, but other people do comment on it, which always surprises me. I don't hear it."

William offered a weak smile. "Trust me, it's there."

Maddie and Gran shared a series of looks. It might be out of context, but somehow they did trust William Blackwell. Also, the man was hurting, and it was up to them to ease his pain if they possibly could.

"After being in America for a few months, I'm getting

homesick for the sound of it. Of course I have Nicholas and. . . ." He replaced his cup with a shaking hand.

"Will you tell Maddie and me a little about yourself?" Gran asked gently.

"Certainly." Leaning back, he clasped his hands over his slightly rounded stomach. "I was born in Devon, and I have one brother. As you may have guessed, I'm a little older than Ava, but when we met it didn't seem to matter. Every day is a blessing when we're together." The corners of his mouth turned down. "I am very sorry that you've been involved in whatever is going on."

Gran nodded. "We appreciate that. We also know that we can't always prevent things from happening. Sometimes it's simply out of our hands and it's how we react that matters."

He nodded thoughtfully.

"How did you inherit a castle?" Maddie asked, genuinely interested.

William smiled. "Now, that is an interesting story. My uncle—my father's eldest brother—was the rightful heir and lived there his whole life. My father was given the family holding in Devon, which was once part of the castle estate. That's where my brother and I were born and raised. We did visit the castle many times, as my father and his brother were extremely close and my uncle was very fond of us. Since he had no children, when he passed away, the castle became mine."

"Were you expecting to inherit it?" Maddie probed.

He shrugged. "I suppose in the back of my mind I knew that would be the case, but my uncle was a very fit man. I didn't think of him passing away anytime soon."

Maddie frowned, wondering if Ethan knew about this. "So, he died suddenly?"

"Very suddenly. A freak accident when he was out shooting," William said with sorrow.

She sat up straighter. "He was murdered?"

William's eyebrows shot up. "I believe it was an accident."

"It would appear that there have been a lot of accidents," Gran noted dryly.

William picked up his cup and drank deeply before replacing it. "That's exactly what Ava said. I apologize, my love. I should have listened to you."

Ava patted his hand. "It doesn't matter now."

He shook his head. "Perhaps I could have prevented Marcus's death if I'd paid attention to your opinions."

Ava made a soothing sound. "Don't upset yourself any more tonight."

William let out a shaky breath. "He'll want to be taken home."

"Yes, of course." Ava squeezed his hand. "We'll see to it as soon as the sheriff says we can leave."

"You're going to live in England," Maddie stated, feeling a wrench she hadn't expected.

"We are," Ava said, shamefaced. "I intended to come and see you both to tell you what we intended. I never meant for you to find out like this, but I couldn't foresee this mess."

Maddie nodded. Her mom was due some good times, even if she had no intention of staying in Maple Falls for longer than she had to. Ava had come for one reason, and it wasn't to be a mom.

"I guess it would be cool to live in a castle," she told her, instead of how she was really feeling.

Gran poured more tea. "Perhaps one day we could

come visit? Once you're settled? It's time I saw my brother again."

Ava's face brightened. "We would love that, wouldn't we, William?"

"You must come anytime you like. You will be welcome and rooms will be available for however long you choose, and that could be permanently."

Even sad, he appeared to genuinely want to please his wife and her family. Maddie watched him for a minute, until something made her ask, "You inherited not only the castle but your family's estate?"

"That's right."

"And your brother wasn't upset by this?" she asked tentatively.

He stiffened. "If you're inferring that Nicholas would want to murder me so that he could gain both properties, let me assure you, he wouldn't. I made a pact with him that once I was ensconced in the castle, he could have our family's land."

"That's very good of you," Gran said.

"Is it? I think it's only fair. A person only needs so much, and I don't have any children to leave my worldly goods to," he insisted.

"Does Nicholas have children?" Maddie pressed.

"He does. A daughter, Amelia. She's a wonderful businesswoman," he said proudly.

Maddie hesitated. "Can I ask how Marcus fits in?"

William sighed. "I don't mind talking about him. Marcus helped out wherever he was needed. He didn't do so well at school but he was eager to please us all. He was my aunt's only child."

This was interesting. "Your father had a sister as well as a brother?"

"Yes. She was the oldest and along with her husband died in the same accident that killed my mother. Marcus is quite a bit younger than us, so becoming an orphan when he was so young was hard for him."

Maddie felt his pain, because it meant that William probably didn't remember much of his mother either. "But you and Marcus were close?"

He nodded enthusiastically. "Marcus had no other family. Everyone concerned was happy for my father to take care of him. When I say we were cousins, I should say that we were more like brothers. He and I were especially inseparable."

Maddie had to ask. "Was Nicholas jealous of your relationship?"

"What? No! He loved Marcus as much as I did. As I still do." He pinched the bridge of his nose once more, and his lips quivered.

Ava glared at Maddie and Gran. "You stop this now! William's lost someone very dear to him. I would think you could both give him some space to deal with this." She stood, and William got to his feet. "We're going to bed."

Gran flinched at the tone. "We're all exhausted. We can talk more in the morning, when the sheriff or his deputy come back."

Wide-eyed, Ava stopped on her way to the stairs. "I thought they said they'd be watching the cottage?"

"They will. I meant when they have a moment tomorrow to come inside. There's no hurry, is there?"

Ava shuddered. "As long as they've not gone home."

Maddie was on her way to get a pillow and blankets from the hall cupboard, and she swung back. "Ethan is a man of his word. He won't let anyone harm us on his watch."

"That's good enough for me. Goodnight, and thank you." William gave them a sad smile and followed Ava up the stairs, a hand in the middle of her back.

Gran waited until she heard a door close. "Well. He seems a thoroughly nice man."

Maddie nodded. "He's been so worried about Mom and just as confused as we are as to who could have killed Marcus. Ava thinks it's the brother, but there's really no evidence apart from his dislike of her. William is just as adamant it's not Nicholas."

"There's certainly more here than meets the eye, and I'm sure half of what William said tonight he hadn't thought to tell Ethan. Good work, sweetheart. Your questions, while I agree with your Mom about them not being perfect timing, revealed so much about motives."

Maddie knew that she could have been more sensitive to William. Unfortunately, like Grandad, once she got her teeth into something she often lost sight of things around her. Very much like baking. A recipe demanded attention to understand it completely, and this murder had many layers. But William Blackwell was a person who was grieving, and she did feel bad about pushing him on the day he found out about Marcus.

"I'll do better tomorrow, I promise. You're right about the motive. Too many people had a lot to gain by William's murder—mainly Nicholas. But who would gain from Mom's? It's kind of an all or nothing scenario. And what if the person who was supposed to drink the poison was actually Marcus?" Maddie's thoughts spun out of control for a moment.

"I appreciate you want to help, sweetheart, but I meant what I said about us all needing sleep. You have a bakery to run tomorrow."

Maddie kissed Gran on the cheek. "As always, you're the voice of reason. Okay, I'm going to have a quick wash and get to bed."

"Good girl. See you in the morning." Gran smiled and headed upstairs.

When Maddie was tucked up on the chaise lounge with moonlight streaming in from the high windows on one side of the sitting room, she closed her eyes and did some deep breathing to relax her.

Sleep proved elusive, and she merely tossed and turned as the grandfather clock in the dining room ticked away the minutes. Lying there, she wondered if the other members of the household were experiencing the same. And was the clock getting louder?

Just as she found a comfortable spot, a scratching noise made her sit up. Unless she was mistaken, the clicking of nails on the kitchen hardwood meant something was headed her way. Maddie swung her legs to the floor, but before she could stand, she was hit in the chest by a considerable weight. A grunt exploded from her as she fell backwards.

"Big Red! Where have you been?" Maddie bit her lip, looking toward the stairs while he pressed his claws warningly into her bare leg. "Sorry. I won't ask," she whispered into his fur.

He leaned forward, green eyes glittering, then licked her cheek and proceeded to get comfortable. The chaise, while big enough for one, had just gotten a great deal smaller. Maddie smothered a chuckle under the blanket. He was a bossy ball of fluff, yet having him beside her might just help her get some sleep. If she could put aside the visual of a hand pointing.

Chapter Twelve

Maddie woke to voices from the kitchen. And a delicious smell. Confused, she lifted her wrist to see her watch and squealed like a stuck pig.

The bakery! With or without an alarm, Maddie generally woke early to get the bread started. With her terrible night's sleep, she had overslept and then some. What was she thinking by still being in bed at this hour? Big Red's absence was also odd. When he woke, he expected food and made sure she was aware of that fact.

Leaping from the chaise, she grabbed her clothes and held them against her. She'd have to change upstairs or in the utility room downstairs. Either place meant passing the kitchen and dining room and whoever might be there.

While she'd be upset for strangers to see her in this state, her worry was focused on the handsome sheriff. She wasn't particularly vain, but he didn't need to see her at her worst. Although, some might argue that he'd already had that pleasure. Thoughts tumbling, she forced herself into action by barreling into the kitchen.

Gran took one look at her face and held up a hand. "No

need to panic. Laura went to work earlier than usual, saying that she and Luke would get things underway."

"That's so kind of her, but I can't leave them to cope shorthanded yet again." Maddie's bakery was her pride and joy, and even knowing Laura and Luke would do just fine, she still felt the weight of responsibility.

Gran sighed. "Laura knows you wouldn't have got much sleep, and it's good practice for her to take charge. Besides, I've kept breakfast for you."

Maddie shook her head stubbornly. "I need to get to the bakery. Where are Mom and William? I should say goodbye."

"They're outside on the front porch with Ethan. You'll need to get by him first." Gran poured a mug of tea and handed it to Maddie.

Maddie raised an eyebrow. "He's still here?"

Gran winked. "Drink that, get dressed, and go see for yourself."

Maddie's cheeks pinked. She probably looked a fright, and Gran was gently prodding her to do something about it. Taking the stairs two at a time, she had a quick wash. There was always a toothbrush here for her but it had been some time since she'd kept any clothes. A shower and change would have to wait until she got back to her apartment over the bakery.

When she got outside, with another cup of tea in one hand and a bacon sandwich in the other—Gran refused to let her out the door without them—she found Ethan leaning against the railing. William occupied Grandad's old rocker, and Ava sat in Gran's. Side by side, they were nodding at Ethan.

"Here she is! Good morning, stepdaughter," William said with pleasure.

Maddie's mouth dropped open, while Ava laughed. Which was kind of weird. Her mom didn't laugh. Well, not properly.

At twenty-nine, Maddie had been treated to many variations of her mother, and none like this. The sound as well as the small crinkles at the corner of her eyes made Ava look several years younger, and Maddie couldn't reconcile this with the woman who always seemed to enjoy being miserable.

"G-g-good morning, William."

"I guess Dad is a bit much to hope for." He smiled at her shocked expression. "Don't mind me. I'm only teasing."

Maddie forced a smile, not sure if he really was teasing, until she noticed Ethan's grin. Completely thrown by the mood, she blurted, "Any news about the murder?" Instantly regretting the outburst when William's smile was replaced by sorrow and Ava glared at her.

"You are not in charge of this investigation. Let the sheriff do his job, and you go on and do yours," her mom said, brooking no argument.

"Right. Sorry. I guess I'll see you later." Maddie walked briskly down the path. She heard footsteps behind her, and a firm grip on her wrist held her back.

"Wait a minute. Are you mad with me?"

She looked down at the worn path. "No, Ethan. I'm mad with myself for the way my emotions are all over the place. I can't get my head around the relationship with Ava and William. I'm trying, but it's not easy after everything that's happened."

A finger tipped her chin so that he could see her face better. "It's only natural to be confused, but don't shut me out."

"I don't mean to. I feel so awkward about everything

that the only thing that keeps me on an even keel is solving this case. Am I weird?"

Both eyebrows shot up. "You? A little."

She smacked his arm, and he grinned.

"As it happens, I kind of like your kind of weird. And if you take notice, you'll see that William and your mom are both struggling but are putting on a show for each other. It's kind of sweet."

Maddie sniffed. "I guess you're right. I honestly think they would take a bullet for each other."

"Okay. I'm not sure we need to go down that road this morning."

She nodded. "I hoped that when I woke up this would all be a dream. I have to get to the bakery now. Will you fill me in on any new details later?"

Ethan flinched. "Hah! It sounds like you and Gran got a darn sight more of those last night than I had the whole of yesterday."

Despite her emotional state, Maddie smiled. "She told you what we discussed?"

He shook his head. "Not Gran—Ava."

"Oh. That's good news. I was going to, but you know. . . seeing them together, the way they are with each other, threw me."

Ethan kissed the tip of her nose, looked around, then kissed her properly. When her knees threatened to buckle, he let her go with a heavy sigh. "One day we won't have to worry about being seen."

"Really?" she rasped.

"Well, I can't promise I'll be as spontaneous as William, but I think I'm mellowing." He winked.

"You are."

Ethan had been very careful about physical contact

when they first started seeing each other, because of his job but also not wanting Maddie to feel pressured. They'd moved on from the awkward phase, and since most people knew that they were a serious item, he'd touch her in public —a hand on her back, an arm across her shoulder. But kissing was still off the table. She didn't mind that. It made the kisses they shared in private more special.

Maddie was about to walk away when she suddenly thought about Honey. Before she could ask, Ethan smiled knowingly.

"She's all safe and sound in your garage. I got Rob to bring her home this morning."

"I'm sure reading minds isn't on your list of credentials, Sheriff."

He grinned. "Not at all. You need a better poker face, sweetheart."

With the endearment echoing in her mind, Maddie practically floated down the road to the bakery.

Chapter Thirteen

Barely in the kitchen door, Maddie got a fright when Angel burst through the bakery door behind her.

"Where's the fire?" she said to her pink-cheeked friend.

"Police everywhere. Late-night comings and goings! You have to tell me everything."

Suzy came through from the shop almost as eagerly. "I thought I heard your voices. There are all these rumors going around about you and the murder, and I've been inundated with calls. I've pleaded no comment, but like Angel, I have to know where things stand and what happened with your mom?"

Laura and Luke were also keen for any updates. Maddie slipped a pristine white apron over her neck, flicking her blonde braid behind her. The shower and change would have to wait.

"Whoa, both of you. I appreciate the need to know or your lives will be unbearable, so let's meet up for lunch. I've been absent from the bakery all morning, and I really have to do some work."

Suzy pulled a face. "Fine, but be prepared. With so many questions, food will be required."

"Just tell us you're doing okay?" Angel asked sincerely, even as her glance slipped away and out to the bakery counter, where a fresh batch of doughnuts glistened.

Always sympathetic to the plight of anyone, Angel couldn't resist food—especially Maddie's. The fact that she never gained so much as a half-pound from testing all Maddie's new recipes and subsisted mainly on doughnuts would annoy the heck out of lesser friends.

Maddie smiled at them. "I'm absolutely fine. Just tired. It was a very late night. I don't have it all worked out yet, but I'll tell you what I do know when we meet up."

Angel pouted. "I guess that will have to do. Luke, could I have my doughnut order, please?"

She had a standing order that was dependent on the day, as flavors would change. Never the amount. It didn't take much to please Angel, but guessing the flavor of the day every morning was certainly one proven way.

Once they'd gone and the shop was empty, Luke and Laura waited at the kitchen counter expectantly while Maddie made tea, already regretting sending Suzy and Angel away. If she was going to have to explain everything several times, this was going to be one very long day.

Sighing, she handed Laura a cup. "I owe you both an apology for being so late this morning."

Laura shook her head. "Don't be silly. Yesterday was pretty horrendous for you. We managed, didn't we, Luke?"

He nodded. "Laura filled me in on what she knew, but I assume there's more to this?"

The bell sounded, signaling a customer. All three frowned, and Maddie saw their exasperation, but customers came first, and Luke was the first to respond.

"Perhaps it would be better if Angel and Suzy came back here and we talked about this together?" Laura suggested.

Maddie nodded. "You're right. I'll text them. They'll both be too busy at work to talk on the phone, and at least there's plenty of food for them." She deliberately tried to keep things lighthearted, otherwise the rest of the morning would be exhausting.

Maddie sent the text, and almost immediately they responded, saying that they'd be happy to come back to the bakery at lunchtime rather than go elsewhere.

"Maddie, Jed would like a word if you don't mind." Luke stood in the entranceway to the shop.

Jed Clayton was Gran's closest friend apart from Mavis Anderson. It was natural he'd be curious about what was happening at the cottage. This was getting out of hand. Ethan might overlook her talking to the Girlz and Luke, who'd helped her on several cases, but giving away details to all and sundry would not go over well.

Maddie made Jed's regular coffee and took it through with a slice of fresh apple pie. He stood as she entered, his eyes drawn to the plate, and he licked his lips.

"Lovely. Did you or your gran make it?" Jed asked her.

"This is all Luke's work," she acknowledged, sitting beside him.

He took a bite and closed his eyes while he chewed for a moment. "Mmmm. The boy can bake."

Luke was loading brownies into the display cabinet, and hearing the compliment, looked very pleased with himself.

Maddie smiled at them both. "He certainly can."

"I daresay you're a good teacher." Jed winked at her. "Like your gran."

109

"I hope so. Although, Gran can still teach me a thing or two."

Jed put down his fork, humor gone like a badly worn coat. "How is she today?"

Maddie clasped her hands on the table. "She's great. Happy to have Mom home."

"Is that so?" Jed asked dubiously. "Well that's good news. Do you think it's appropriate for me to visit when she has a houseful?"

"Jed, you know you and Sissy are welcome anytime."

That helped to make him less anxious. They both looked outside to where Sissy lay tied to the post Maddie had provided for the pets. It was used every day, as was the bowl of fresh water placed beside it. The glossy coat of the red setter shone in the morning sunlight. Sissy raised her head at the sound of her name, tail thumping the ground.

"Then we'll make our way down there after this pie. I've been cooped up at home for a couple of days with a cold, but I felt so much better that I walked into town. That's when I heard Ava was home."

Tall and thin, Jed was older than Gran by a couple of years. They'd known each other most of their lives and both were incredibly sprightly. He walked for miles and would have only stayed away to spare Gran and their friends at the community center from his germs. Now he seemed disappointed that he'd heard the news second- or perhaps third-hand.

"You let me know if you need a ride home after your visit," Maddie told him.

"That's very kind, but I think I can manage." He patted her hand.

When several more customers came in, Maddie left him to his pie and helped serve for a while. After that she ran upstairs to shower and change. When she got back to the kitchen, she decided to make a batch of eclairs, since everything else appeared to be done.

She felt incredibly lucky to have found not one but two interns who had the same passion that she did for baking and in wanting the bakery to flourish.

As soon as she told them what she was baking, Luke and Laura took turns watching and serving customers. Having grasped the basics early in their employment, their excitement over anything Maddie made for the first time delighted her.

When the choux pastry was ready to pipe, she let them take turns. The result was hilarious and just what she needed to lift her spirits.

"With all the frosting I've been doing lately, you'd think I could pipe an eclair. I'm guessing that these aren't for the shop?" Laura asked when her strip of pastry took on the shape of a banana.

Maddie bit back a laugh. Encouragement was what they needed. "Not today. We all need more practice. I'm hoping to tempt Angel away from her doughnuts on occasion and also have something new in the shop. These can be for lunch today for all of us."

"I can't wait to try them. I've never had one," Luke said.

"Really?" Maddie was surprised.

He shrugged. "The diner only serves pie for dessert. Before you opened Maple Lane Bakery, there was no place in town to get eclairs or any of the treats you bake. If it hadn't been for Gran and the internet, I wouldn't know most of this stuff existed."

Maddie had forgotten this. Having worked in New York, she was fortunate to have tried many different cakes, pastries, and biscuits. Not that she was convinced any other cookies or cakes were a match for Gran's, and she was pretty sure that most of Maple Falls would agree with her.

They were kept busy with customers, especially as lunchtime came. At one o'clock, Angel and Suzy arrived.

"I have to be back at the school by two for a meeting," Suzy told them.

Angel nodded, already headed to the kitchen. "I have to do a color then too, but Beth will do the shampoo for me if I'm running late."

Laura put fresh tea and coffee pots on the table, alongside the plates and tea sets Gran donated when Maddie first opened the shop. When they were seated, Luke placed fresh sandwiches and a quiche in front of them.

Angel looked down at the food, then glanced around the kitchen.

"Looking for something?" Maddie asked, suppressing a grin.

"Lunch looks nice, but aren't we having something sweet?"

"You already had your doughnuts, so I figured you wouldn't want anything else," Maddie teased.

The unhappy look was enough for Luke and Laura to lose it, and Maddie laughed with them on her way to the counter, where a cake cover hid the surprise. Underneath was the plate of eclairs, now covered in chocolate and stuffed with fresh whipped cream. She brought it to the table, and Angel gasped.

"Oh, my! Are they eclairs?"

"They are, and they can sit right here until we're ready for them," Maddie told her, about to place them on the far side.

"I don't think so." Angel glared at her.

Maddie knew not to argue with the sugarholic, and the

plate didn't make it any farther before Angel had one in her hand. Without any pretense at ladylike behavior, she bit into it, rolling her eyes with a contented sigh.

"This is heaven. Suzy, you must have one."

Suzy ate a sandwich, watching the eclairs. Shaking her head, she dragged her regretful gaze to Maddie. "Maybe later, if she leaves any. Perhaps you should put some aside for the rest of us."

"Rude," said Angel, dabbing at her mouth with a napkin before taking another large bite.

Suzy grimaced before turning her focus on why they were here. "Okay, Maddie. Spill."

Maddie sighed. "You all heard what Mom said, apart from Luke. She came back to get away from a bad situation. She's now married and her husband, William, seems very nice. I met him last night at the hospital in Destiny when we went for Mom to identify the body."

All eyes were glued to her, and Maddie, appreciating that they would be here a while, took a minute to eat a sandwich.

"And who was it?" Suzy asked.

"It was William's cousin. They were very close, so it's hit him hard. Mom's pretty upset too," Maddie explained.

Suzy and Angel shared a look, and Maddie could guess that they were thinking that the Ava they knew didn't have attachments to people.

"What does Ethan think of everything?" Suzy asked.

"He doesn't know what to think. I'm sure he'll have some ideas, but we haven't had any time to talk," Maddie explained.

"He probably wants to keep some of the clues to himself, knowing that this would happen." Angel waved a hand around the table.

The others smiled.

Suddenly, Suzy grimaced. "Talk about bad timing. Gran's party is just around the corner, and this happens."

Maddie nodded. "I know. I wanted to talk to Jed this morning, but he was off to see Gran, so I thought I better not."

"You'll still go ahead with it?" Laura asked, looking astonished.

Maddie had thought about it last night along with everything else. "I don't think so. Once I talk to Ethan and see if it's safe to do so, we can get on with our plans when we think it's appropriate. There will be a funeral to organize first. Besides, we could make it for later date."

Angel's hand halted in midair as it reached for another eclair. "Why would it not be safe?"

"The murderer is still out there," Maddie reminded her.

Luke paled. "But he or she isn't after Gran, are they?"

Maddie chewed her lip for a moment. "If they want to hurt Ava, they might try to do so through Gran."

"That's despicable!" Laura slapped the table, making them all jump.

"Anyone trying to hurt Gran would be lower than a snake!" Luke added furiously.

Maddie's appetite disappeared. She sipped her tea while listening to the Girlz and Luke discussing the murderer and how whoever it was better not mess with Gran. It was humbling to hear her friends talk this way. The love and affection they had for Gran was so obvious.

"We can't let a stranger ruin her big day like this," Suzy growled.

Maddie decided it was time to calm things down before Suzy got out the pitchforks and rallied the town.

"I know how you all feel, but Marcus being murdered is

bad enough, regardless of the fact that we don't know him. Having the party might draw the murderer out. I don't imagine Ethan wants to encourage that, and nor do I. Hopefully he'll be caught as soon as possible, then we can carry on with our plans."

"I guess you're right. We can have a party anytime, but there's only one Gran," Suzy acknowledged graciously.

Maddie smiled at her friend. "Actually, that's a nice way to look at it. It will make me feel better about not going ahead."

Suzy gave her a side-eye look. "Sounds like you've already given up?"

"Not yet, but I know Ethan won't risk anyone's safety. Not even yours."

Suzy snorted. "I knew there was a reason to have him around that wasn't all about his good looks."

Maddie snorted. Ethan wasn't exactly one of the Girlz, but he was the next best thing when she needed someone to talk to. Always willing to help any of them, he never objected when he wasn't included in their Girlz time.

The perfect boyfriend, except for when he was looking for a murderer. It might be his job but she didn't like him to be in danger either. She tried not to let the possibility bother her, and at least with the Girlz around her she wasn't quite so scared or anxious.

Chapter Fourteen

"*A*fternoon, beautiful."

Ethan arrived as Maddie was preparing for the cooking class she'd postponed until tonight. Having thought about him all afternoon, she ran into his arms. He squeezed her in that way that stole her breath and made her insides turn as gooey as a molten lava cake.

"Tough day?" he breathed softly in her ear, before setting her down. Then he gave Big Red a scratch as the large cat wound around his legs.

She smiled at their mutual affection. "Not compared to yesterday. I've just missed you, and my head won't be quiet trying to figure all this out."

"I know what you mean. We got back the reports on William, Nicholas, and Marcus Blackwell."

"Already?"

"I called in a favor. You're not the only one with New York connections." He waggled an eyebrow.

Having lived there for a couple of years, Maddie had a good friend she'd worked with in the city. They rang each other periodically with updates about their lives. Ethan knew they were long conversations—and the next one would be even longer!

"Very funny. What did the report say?"

"William is clean. Nicholas and Marcus, almost. There have been links to a few shady deals."

She shook her head. "Wow. I'm glad William is above-board. I wonder if he knew Marcus was dodgy. After listening to Mom, I don't think he would think his cousin or his brother capable of anything underhanded."

"It sounds like Marcus, although devoted to William, had a few recent business dealings with Nicholas."

Maddie made coffee for him. "Maybe that's why he was killed. What kind of deals?"

He sat at the table and gratefully took his mug. "They supplied cars to people—expensive cars."

"Stolen cars?"

He shrugged. "Nothing's proven yet, but several have been impounded."

"I don't understand."

"It's still unclear what was happening or who was responsible for which part of the scheme. Nicholas was having money problems because of deals falling over and has been selling anything he can get his hands on back in England. Marcus had connections in New York. According to William's secretary, who's home now, Marcus and Nicholas had a heated discussion about whether to involve William. Apparently, it didn't go well."

"They had a physical fight?"

Ethan nodded and drank deeply. "That might explain the bruise on the side of Marcus's face."

Maddie's chin lifted. "I don't recall a bruise. So you think Marcus was dragged into this unwittingly?"

He shrugged. "Perhaps."

"Where is Nicholas?"

"We're still searching for him. He hasn't been back to the apartment he leased next to Ava and William since William left the hospital."

Maddie tapped her thigh. "That's interesting. I wonder if he's in Maple Falls too?"

Ethan grabbed her hand. "Let's not panic just yet."

Suddenly, Maddie had the impression that Ethan had other information. In light of other questions she had, she decided to let it go for now. "I'll try not to. You said William's secretary told the police about the fight. Were all the staff as willing to talk?"

Ethan shrugged. "It's my impression that many wealthy people don't actually see their key staff members. Literally. It's like they're part of the furniture and can't hear conversations or see what's going on. I never met him, but I imagine that the secretary only confided in the police when he was given no option."

Maddie shook her head with disbelief. "That's awful and kind of crazy." Maddie also wondered how her mom would have coped with having people around her all day and how she might have treated them.

He smiled ruefully. "Yet helpful for us. And by that I don't mean you. Can you keep this information under your hat for now? I'd hate for any of the people we've spoken with to get in trouble or worse."

"Not even the Girlz?"

"No one just now," he said firmly.

"Okay. It'll be hard."

He made a rude noise. "I know."

"What about Gran and Ava?" she almost pleaded, needing someone else to talk this over with.

This time he shrugged. "Since they know as much as

you, I guess it can't hurt. I've told them not to make any calls and to stay at the cottage for today."

Maddie frowned. "What then? Where will they go?"

"I was thinking about your cabin?" he mentioned casually.

She tilted her head. "That might be a plan if you think Nicholas won't know about it."

"The thing is, because we don't know for sure it's him, someone else could be out there watching any of the family. It would be too easy to follow."

Maddie shivered. "That's what I'm fearful of. Is someone at the cottage now to protect them?"

"Rob's there. Gran's keeping him fed and he's happy for now, but he can't be with them twenty-four hours a day."

"I could go feed his puppies and take them for a walk before my class starts, if that would help?"

Ethan gave her a funny look. "I think he's asked Laura."

Maddie couldn't help the grin that spread across her face. "Well, it's about time."

"Now don't go all matchmakery on me. It hasn't been clear sailing between the two of them, so let them work it out for themselves."

"I just want them to be as happy as we are."

Ethan gave her a megawatt smile. "I'm sure if it's meant to be, they will end up together." Then he kissed her several times, driving any thoughts but those of being in his arms from her mind. When he released her, they were both short of breath.

"I'd better get back to the station and see if there's any updates," he managed.

"Alright. The class might run late tonight if Angel shows up, so I'll see you tomorrow."

He shook his head. "One of these days, we're going to get some time together."

She ran a hand through his hair. "I look forward to that, Sheriff."

He sighed, kissed her one last time, then left her to continue setting up. With that done, she had a moment or two to have a quick bite and feed Big Red before taking him upstairs.

Mavis Anderson and Nora Beatty arrived first. One as bright as sunshine, and the other as drab as a winter sky. They were friends and lived at the retirement community on the edge of town. Neither drove, so they were dropped off by Bernie.

He waved to her from the roadside after making sure his charges were dispatched without issue. Mavis, talking a mile a minute, entered the kitchen followed by Nora.

"I'm saying he drives too fast," the latter grumbled.

"You're too hard on the boy. Bernie has always taken care with us." Mavis said in her singsong voice.

"Boy? Woman, you need glasses. Bernie's well past that age and more."

"Thirties is young to me, Nora."

"Hummpf!"

"Good evening, ladies." Maddie couldn't help thinking, not for the first time, what an odd couple they were for close friends.

Mavis hugged her. "Hello, dear. How is your gran? We've been hearing all kinds of things, and I'm sorry to say none of it good."

"You can thank me for holding her back from coming here first thing this morning," Nora stated self-righteously. She removed her coat and scarf, handing them to Maddie. "I suspect it didn't keep her from making a call."

"You want to know too. Or have you forgotten grilling Bernie like Sherlock Homes?" Mavis giggled.

She removed her hand-knitted cardigan to slip the apron Maddie provided over a tartan skirt and floral blouse. Apart from Angel, Mavis was the happiest person Maddie had ever met, and her delight in everything was infectious.

Nora made another rude sound, and Maddie intervened.

"Gran's fine. As you've heard, Mom's visiting and there was a death in her husband's family, so they're tied up with that right now."

Nora's eyebrows danced up and down. "Yes, we heard about the sudden marriage. And the body. Just how is it related to Ava?"

Maddie felt her smile tighten. "It was her husband's cousin."

Mavis tutted. "How sad."

"A new husband and family out of the blue. That must feel odd to you and your Gran." Nora watched her carefully.

With the class starting soon, Maddie didn't have the time or inclination to do battle with Nora when she was in this challenging mood.

"It began as a lovely surprise." It was a white lie, but Maddie didn't want to have the shock of it resounding around town. "I don't have a lot of family, as you know," she added.

"You have all of us," Mavis declared, a sheen to her eyes as she hugged Maddie again.

A lump lodged in Maddie's throat. Everyone knew her situation, and she had to agree that many of Maple Falls' residents indeed felt like family. Mavis and Jed had been there for Gran when Ava left and before that, when

Grandad passed away. They had also been there for Maddie, and she would never forget their kindness. Even Nora, in her own way.

"More than enough, if you ask me," Nora chimed in, but now there was a distinct hoarseness to her voice.

Fortunately, they were thwarted in getting too emotional by the arrival of the other members of the group.

"You're looking gorgeous as ever, Mrs. Anderson. And you, Ms. Beatty." Chris Jamieson, owner of the appliance store, made Mavis giggle like a schoolgirl, while Nora took a seat and glared at his familiarity.

Noah Jackson, the local yoga instructor and DJ, was quieter but just as friendly.

"Hey, ladies. Maddie, how's Gran?"

A lot of people called her that instead of her given name of Beatrice, and somehow it just seemed right. "She's great," Maddie answered

When she was asked, yet again, about the body, she wished she had the answers on replay. Small towns were wonderful and frustrating in equal measure. Generally people wanted to help, but there was a sense of entitlement about knowing everyone's business that was a struggle to accept.

Perhaps growing up in this environment gave Maddie the same thirst for knowledge and drive for wanting to solve crimes. That, and having a grandad who liked to dig around, personally and professionally.

Finally, she got them all settled and was just about to start when Angel opened the door.

"Is there still room for me tonight? I hear the recipe was designed especially for sweet tooths." She winked.

Maddie beckoned her in. "You know that you're always welcome."

The men jumped up and made room. Nora tutted and Mavis fussed, so it was another five minutes before they could begin.

"Let's have a quick read through the recipe before we get into it."

With that done, they headed to the stove elements with their pots of butter and began making the choux. Adding flour, they had to energetically beat until they all had a mixture to the right consistency. Or, as near to it as possible.

Maddie patiently showed them how to fill the piping bags, and with various success in making straight lines, they managed to make several eclairs each.

Once the trays were loaded, they were placed in the cabinet-style oven on several shelves. Her bakers stood back proudly.

"I'll make tea and coffee," she told them. "Using the recipe you already have in your notebook, go ahead and make the frosting and whip the cream."

Angel was in her element, having done them in previous classes. "I can't believe I remembered how to do this!"

Mavis's couldn't take her eyes from the rising eclairs, and her excitement was catching.

"Are they done?" she asked several times. "They look done."

Finally, to her delight, Maddie agreed. "Carefully remove your tray and place it here on the counter. We'll have the tea while we wait for them to cool."

Noah licked his lips. "Won't they be better warm?"

"Silly. You can't put cream and frosting on something warm." With a laugh, Mavis tapped him on the arm, and he almost lost his tray.

"Careful, Mavis. The trays are hot, and we don't want

any burns," Maddie warned.

Mavis was immediately contrite. "Sorry, Noah."

"No harm, no foul. Let me get yours out," he offered.

"Then I'll pour your coffee." Mavis beamed.

Nora tutted once more, but looked extremely pleased with her eclairs.

Having checked them all, Maddie had to agree that Nora's batch was the most even in height and length and the straightest. Although she had more baking experience, Angel had never made eclairs, so Maddie was especially proud of her friend, whose effort was almost as good.

When they were cooled, Maddie showed them how to hollow out the middle and fill them with cream, then to frost each one. While they were not as messy as children she'd taught, the counter was soon speckled in chocolate drips and cream.

Angel lifted an eclair. "I'm sorry, Maddie. I have to eat one right now."

"You can eat as many as you want—they're all yours. Here's some take-out containers just in case you can't manage every one of them." Maddie winked at the group.

When they'd cleaned up, Maddie saw them to the door. "See you all next week."

Mavis hugged her unexpectedly. "Take care, dear, and give my love to Gran. I won't bother her while she has family staying who need her right now, but if I can help in any way, please tell her to call. Otherwise, I hope to see her at the center real soon."

Maddie's heart tugged. Mavis would be desperate to see Gran, but it wasn't up to her to encourage visitors. And with her mom's moods, it didn't seem fair to put this sweet woman in her way.

"I'll tell her," she promised.

Bernie waited at the curb and jumped out to open the doors for Nora and Mavis. "It always smells so good around here," he called to her.

Maddie laughed. "For a bakery, that's good to hear. Drive safe, and I'll see you all next week." The fact was, she would be bound to see most of them before the next class, and by then she hoped life would have calmed down.

Angel waited by the counter. "Are you sleeping here tonight?"

"Yes. I thought about going back to the cottage, but it doesn't make sense when I need to be back here so early in the morning. The chaise is not as comfortable as it looks either."

Angel chewed her lip. "You'd be safer there."

Though touched by her friend's concern, Maddie didn't feel up to the walk in the dark or another argument with her mom. "I'll make sure that I lock up, and I do have Big Red."

Angel frowned. "Promise to call if you need me?"

"I promise, but I think my boyfriend might be better equipped," Maddie teased.

"Well, that goes without saying, sugar, but that man is all around town lately."

Angel was right about that. Still, Maddie refused to give in to a fear that probably was unwarranted, since she wasn't likely to be anyone's target. Was she?

"Ethan's busy trying to find the murderer, which he'll do," she stated.

Angel hovered at the door. "Let's hope he does so soon. I'll see you in the morning."

They hugged, then Maddie watched Angel walk two doors down the street to her apartment above the salon.

She was about to close her door when she heard Angel scream.

Chapter Fifteen

Heart pounding, Maddie ran as fast as she could. Imagining all kinds of terrible things happening to her best friend, she was overcome with relief when she found her friend lying at the bottom of the few steps, holding her ankle.

"What happened?" Maddie asked, gasping for breath.

Angel groaned, speaking through clenched teeth as she pointed to the right. "I saw someone over by that shrub."

"Who was it?" Maddie took a step toward the greenery before thinking better of it and returning to Angel's side.

"It's too dark to see, but he didn't look friendly. His eyes were so cold."

A chill ran up Maddie's back. "Are you sure it was a man if you couldn't see them clearly?"

Angel sniffed. "I do think I can tell the difference."

Maddie hid a smile. "I meant it may not have been a person."

"Oh no," Angel wailed.

"What is it?" Instantly on high alert, Maddie scanned the darkness.

"My eclairs." Angel sniffed again. "They're ruined."

Maddie looked down in wonder. Angel must be suffering from shock. Maddie took the house keys from her friend's lap, opened the back door, and flicked the light switch. Angel pulled herself up by the railing, and Maddie bit back an inappropriate laugh. The outside light, less bright, had hid the mess. The eclairs had fallen from the container and been squashed, covering the steps in cream and chocolate frosting—and they had done the same to Angel.

For emphasis, a big lump fell from the top of Angel's head. She squealed as it landed on the floor when she stepped inside the back of the salon.

On cue, Ethan ran up the path. "Are you two okay?"

"Angel fell when someone gave her a fright. They were apparently over there." Maddie nodded at the bush.

"That's right, and he ran off that way." Angel pointed up the street towards the library.

"Jumping the wall?" Ethan asked.

Each of the four backyards was encased in low stone walls at the front with metal gates, but the ones at the sides were much higher. Maddie felt as unsure as Ethan sounded.

Angel gave him a perplexed look. "He must have."

"We would have heard the gate, so there is no other option," Maddie offered as consolation. "Let's get you comfortable."

With her arms around their shoulders, they managed to help Angel hop upstairs to her apartment and over to the pale blue couch. Ethan pulled up a chair for her to put her foot on.

Angel smiled her thanks, but he didn't acknowledge her, his mind clearly on something else.

"What's wrong?" Maddie asked.

He came back to the room with a start. "It's puzzling me that I didn't see anyone, since I came from that direction."

"He could have gone anywhere after that. Perhaps down between the library and the butcher shop?"

Ethan nodded. "You're probably right. I'll get Deputy Jacobs to come by and bring more torches so we can have a better look."

Maddie collected ice from the freezer, wrapping it in a small towel before laying it on Angel's already bruised ankle.

"I'll help if you like?" she said to Ethan.

"I think you should get back to the bakery and stay inside until we make sure no one's around." Ethan turned to Angel. "Could you see what he looked like?"

Angel shook her head. "Someone moving in the shadows was all I noticed."

"Okay. After I see Maddie home, I'll come back to get a statement." He gave Angel a peculiar look. "Ahh, is that what I think it is?" Ethan pointed to her hair.

With the ice perched precariously on her ankle, Angel took another cloth from Maddie, giving him an exasperated glance. "Don't even think about criticizing my baking. My eclairs were divine."

It wasn't clear if Angel was more upset over the eclairs or the fright she'd just had. If it weren't for that shocking fact, seeing her immaculate friend in such a state would incite Maddie to hysterical laughter.

It took all her willpower not to succumb when Angel's attempt to clean herself up without a mirror had cream and chocolate smearing into a worse concoction. Maddie forced herself to offer a straight-faced positive note.

"They were wonderful, and you are quite capable of making more, but you don't have to. I'm teaching Laura and

Luke to make them, and we'll be stocking them in the bakery from next week."

"Now I won't know whether I should buy doughnuts or eclairs," Angel said as she looked out into the night.

From where they sat on the couch, there was zero visibility of the gardens or paths apart from where the light of a few streetlamps touched them. Ethan stood at the side of the window looking up and down Plum Place while he called in the alert.

When he was done, he turned back to them and frowned. "Will you be okay here on your own, Angel?"

"Of course. It'll take more than a peeping Tom to scare me off."

"I can stay over," Maddie said, wondering if Angel believed that's what it really was.

Angel raised an eyebrow. "No, you'll be happier at home, and a 5:00a.m wake up doesn't excite me."

Maddie snorted, then made sure Angel had everything she needed, including a blanket in case she decided to sleep on the couch. With a kiss on the cheek, she left her friend with a drink, snacks, and the remote for the TV. She turned all the lights on while Ethan drew the curtains.

When they were outside, Ethan checked Angel's door was locked, dropping her spare key in his pocket. Back at her place, all the lights blazed just as she'd left them. Big Red sat on the bottom stair. He mewled—an unpleasant sound.

"Someone's annoyed with you." Ethan smirked.

"I didn't mean to leave him behind. The door must have slammed after me." Maddie called the cross cat, but he turned his head.

"That's you told off. Now, I'm going to check around to make sure it's just you and grumpy here."

Maddie hadn't given a thought to anyone coming inside. "Big Red wouldn't be sitting here, grumpy or otherwise, if there was a stranger in the bakery or apartment."

"I guess that's true, but humor me?"

She grabbed his arm, a sudden fear hitting her. What if this were a ruse to get the sheriff and deputies away from the cottage? "If you're here, who's at Gran's?"

Ethan smiled reassuringly. "It turns out that Jerry Sims has enough credentials to help out."

She let him go, wondering that her mom knew people like Jerry and William. How polar opposites could those men be?

Ethan was only gone a few minutes before he clomped back down the stairs. Big Red gave his foot a swipe, but Ethan was wise to his tricks and stepped over him before taking a quick glance in the bakery.

"All safe and secure?"

"It will be when you lock the door behind me."

Maddie followed him to the door. "Will you let me know if you find anyone?"

Ethan gave her a quick peck on the cheek. "I'm sure whoever it is will be long gone, but if I do and it's not too late, I'll be sure to call you."

She knew that was his best offer, but incredibly tired as she was, Maddie knew she wasn't going to sleep. Bravado only went so far. They were all troubled, and as she went upstairs, staying here by herself didn't seem as palatable as it had when Ethan was here.

From upstairs in her apartment sitting room, Maddie had a good view of the back of this block and across to the fields on the other side of the road. Her bedroom window on the right-hand corner of the apartment had another outlook. The park was partially visible due to a solar light over a bench. Situated on the edge of the grass, both were shadowed by a large maple tree.

Her own and Angel's house lights, plus the several lights arcing around the other backyards in Plum Place, brightened up the area.

It made her feel a little safer, but the whole business was as troubling as it was confusing. A dark-haired stranger could be Nicholas Blackwell, or it could be someone else. Or maybe it was a stray dog? Yet Angel had seemed so adamant it was a man.

If it was Marcus's murderer, why would they choose tonight and Angel's place in particular to show themselves? For a start, Angel hadn't met William yet and had no vested interest in Maddie's stepfather or the castle. Ava wasn't in town often enough for her to be the key. If it wasn't about either of them, then someone else was set on scaring Angel, which made no sense at all.

Once it might have, but Angel's ex-husband had turned his life around. Maddie couldn't imagine him going back to the man he'd been after all they'd been through, and he wouldn't hurt Angel.

Suddenly, two shadows peeled away from the others and came up her walk, their arms around each other. Maddie ran downstairs, almost tripping over Big Red, who was just as interested to find out who the arrivals were. Cautiously she peered through the window to find Angel with someone who didn't wear a uniform. Emitting a gasp, Maddie quickly opened the door.

Detective Jones nodded. "Sorry to bother you at this time of night, Ms. Flynn."

"I can't imagine anyone is sleeping around here," she told him, while raising her eyebrow at Angel.

"The detective insists I come stay the night while they

check out my place. Inside and out. I did explain that the door was still locked when I got home, but he won't listen." Angel waved a hand theatrically.

The detective stared stoically at Angel, who was decidedly flushed. Maddie hid a smile. These two were so darn cute. They couldn't see how obvious their attraction for each other was to the rest of Maple Falls.

"Actually, I'd be grateful for the company. I have a bad feeling I can't shake, and having you here will help take my mind off it," Maddie admitted.

"The whole experience is unsettling. I guess if we can't sleep, we'll have plenty to talk about." Angel glanced at the detective.

"Anything I should know about?" he asked in the abrupt way he had.

Angel sniffed. "Not really."

Maddie helped the detective get her upstairs and settled in a severe case of déjà vu. The tall, fair man was always professional, but Angel seemed to be his Achilles heel, and he seemed not to care for that at all.

"I don't like secrets," he said as he hovered over Angel.

"Seems to me that only works one way, Detective," she sniffed.

They were like two boxers circling each other, yet there was this electricity in the air, and Maddie couldn't stand the tension.

"We're fixing to have a surprise party for Gran's seventieth in less than two weeks if it's not too dangerous."

The detective's eyebrows shot up into his hairline. "Right now, I'd put those plans on hold until we find our man."

"If we do find him—"

He cut her off. "I wasn't including you in the hunt, Ms. Flynn."

"A slip of the tongue, nothing more," Maddie told him, noting that he didn't look convinced. "But we would include you in the invites when we do have the party, now that you spend so much time in Maple Falls."

Her buttering up served only to manufacture a couple of worry lines on his forehead. Hurriedly placing the overnight bag he still had on his arm beside Angel, he retreated with a cough. Frightened wasn't the right word to describe the look he gave them. She doubted the detective was capable of being so, but he was certainly wary.

"If it makes you feel uncomfortable, forget she mentioned it," Angel told him.

"Thank you for the invite, Ms. Flynn. However, I do feel it might be unprofessional."

"How on earth is having a party with friends unprofessional?" Angel scoffed.

He seemed startled by the term. "It wouldn't be, but we haven't known each other long enough, surely?"

"A year seems long enough." Angel tilted her head to the side. "You don't strike me as the kind of person who pays attention to what people think of him."

"I can assure you, I don't," he said stiffly.

"Then you'll come."

It wasn't a question. The staunch detective was outmaneuvered, and the realization as it hit was fascinating to watch.

He took a large breath. "If everything works out and the case is closed by then, I would be happy to attend."

"Good. Off you go. I'll see you tomorrow," Angel said, her lips twitching.

His face hinted at amusement before falling into a confused look. "Good evening."

Like Ethan, he waited until Maddie locked the door before leaving.

Wanting to grill Angel on the frisson between the couple, Maddie had to wait, as the phone rang just as she got back upstairs. It was Gran wanting to know what all the ever-loving police were doing down her way and was she in danger?

By the time she assured Gran that they were safe, Angel had taken her bag and hobbled down the hall. Maddie found her in the spare bedroom, where she'd flopped on the bed.

"So, how did it come about that the detective was at your house?" Maddie asked casually.

"Ethan called him. Steve's staying in Maple Falls so he can talk to your mom and William in the morning. When he heard that there was a prowler, he rushed right over."

"And straight to your place?" Maddie kept her voice even, but her ears had pricked up at the "Steve."

Angel checked her manicured nails. "I'm sure it wasn't like that. He probably saw all the lights and figured my place was a good place to start."

"Perhaps he wanted to check on you personally?" Maddie could barely contain her laughter.

Angel blushed, fussing with a nail polish chip that may or may not be real. Finally, she looked up and answered more honestly. "I guess I should be flattered if that's the case?"

Maddie grinned. "I think you should at least entertain the idea."

"Am I crazy?" Angel asked resignedly.

"To have feelings for Steve?"

Angel lifted her head as if to argue but shrugged instead. "If you remember, sugar, I did swear off men."

Maddie flinched. With a horrible marriage that involved drunken abuse, Angel had come a long way from her deep skepticism about men when it came to herself. Oddly, for others she could always see the happy ever after.

"That was completely understandable at the time. But your ex-husband is in a good space, and you've forgiven him for all the bad times. I'd say now is the perfect time to move on."

Angel sighed dramatically. "But Steve's so . . . ."

"Controlled? Annoyingly so?"

Angel nodded and they grinned at each other.

"Unless you want to sleep, I'll make us tea while we wait for any news."

"Tea would be lovely." Angel pulled herself to a sitting position and propped a couple of pillows behind her head. The ankle looked less puffy, but while the kettle boiled, Maddie fetched another ice pack just in case.

Still thinking about Steve Jones and his attraction to her friend, Maddie had noticed the faraway look in Angel's eyes. Considering how much denial had been invested over many months regarding anything between them, this was indeed a huge flag of capitulation. Maddie didn't choose to squander it.

She brought two cups into the bedroom, placing them on the small bedside table. After fetching Angel's bag, Maddie sat in a chair opposite the bed.

"Wouldn't you agree, in the time you've known Detective Jones he's softened quite a lot?" Maddie wiped her hand across the cabinet, checking for dust.

Angel sipped thoughtfully. "I guess he has, but it shouldn't be so difficult to get through to a man."

"It depends on what you want him to know or feel about you. Perhaps that's why you like him, because unlike every other man hereabouts, he hasn't fallen at your feet," Maddie suggested. "Besides, I suspect the persona these lawmen adopt so they can be seen as tough is like a Lawman 101."

Angel wasn't at all offended. "I like tough, but I also like gentle."

"Most women do, but you'll never know if he can be both unless you give him a chance." Maddie sighed, thinking of Ethan. She had very nearly not given him a second chance and hated to think about not being with him.

"I'll think about it," Angel said.

"That's all I'm saying. Besides, you'll need a partner for the party."

Angel snorted so bad, tea came out her nostrils. "You are terrible," she gasped.

"But you love me." Maddie laughed, giving her a handful of tissues from the box on the bedside table.

"That goes without saying, but I swear our sheriff is having an adverse effect on you."

"I like to blame him too, but he does like a laugh. Even if he doesn't always get our sense of humor!" Maddie laughed harder. The Girlz were notorious for teasing each other, and she was as guilty as any of them. Even Laura, the most sensitive of all of them, was learning to accept their often irreverent sense of humor.

An hour later, no one had stopped by, so Angel and Maddie went to bed, accepting that their men would protect them and grateful that the latter part of the evening had helped to disperse some of the trauma of strangers in their midst.

Chapter Sixteen

On Wednesday morning, Ethan turned up as Maddie loaded bread into the oven. It was always an early start in the bakery, but Maddie still felt guilty about not being available to help yesterday morning and was determined to get a good start today and take the pressure off her interns.

Once he was inside the door, Ethan kissed her deeply.

"I've missed you," he said into her ear.

She was flushed from the oven—mostly—and his breath made her shiver, in the nicest possible way. "Me too," she whispered back. "The funny thing is that we've probably seen each other more in the last few days than we did the whole week before."

He grimaced. "It's not quite the same as being together with no drama unfolding around us. That fact should in no way encourage you to get involved in this case just to see me," he teased as he let her go.

She screwed up her nose. "Ahh, since it revolves around my mom, I am involved. Anyway, you seem very chipper. Coffee?"

He nodded, but didn't sit, leaning instead against the counter as he watched her. Big Red took the opportunity to lie across his feet like a rug.

"I got an email this morning. Actually, it came late yesterday but I missed it. Nicholas Blackwell is no longer a suspect. Apparently, he's been in hospital himself. He was admitted the day William left."

Maddie was hoping for good news, but this confused her. "Wow! What happened to him?"

"He was poisoned too and was incapable of being in Maple Falls when Marcus died."

She handed him a mug. "You seem weirdly happy about that."

He gave a wry smile. "Admittedly, this doesn't solve the case, but it does narrow down suspects. While I'm not exactly celebrating, for a certain cute baker and her family's safety, it does make me very relieved that one of your new family members isn't trying to kill another of them." He tucked a tendril of hair behind her ear. "You're very important to me."

She smiled at his sweetness. He'd never spoken this way when they were teenage boyfriend and girlfriend, and certainly not when they first reconnected in Maple Falls. But over the last few months, he'd become increasingly comfortable with declarations like this, and she never got tired of hearing them.

Maddie's skin tingled when he leaned so close his arm brushed hers, and their lips touched gently. Then her eyes widened. "Wait a minute. What about Marcus and the woman?"

Ethan sighed, used to how her mind jumped around. "Like I said, the case isn't solved, but I will say that

Marcus's death doesn't appear to be linked to the poisonings. The autopsy is today, so I'll find out more then."

Maddie gaped. "So, William was right about his brother?"

"It would appear so."

"Mom was so sure. Unless Nicholas drank the same poison to take the heat off himself." Maddie wracked her brain for solutions.

Ethan merely raised an eyebrow. "That's a little extreme, don't you think?"

"Maybe, but if he's in a hospital he could be assured of help." Maddie groaned, and Ethan took her hand.

"Don't get upset, sweetheart. We'll find out what happened eventually."

Maddie grimaced. "There's still the man in Angel's garden."

"I know Angel was certain she saw a person, yet there were no footprints. We'll ask around some more, but I'm not convinced anyone was there." Ethan didn't meet her eyes.

Maddie folded her arms. "Angel wouldn't lie, and she'll be cross if you don't believe her."

He grimaced. "I know. I don't look forward to telling her my thoughts."

"Well, apart from that, I guess there's nothing to be done for now."

"I'll assume you mean nothing for you and the Girlz to do?"

She had the good grace to blush, and it was his turn to groan.

"I knew it. Okay, here's an idea. With no other suspects and Nicholas in hospital, why don't you go ahead and organize the party for Gran?"

"Seriously? Wouldn't it be bad taste with the funeral for Marcus this Friday?"

"Once I hear back from the autopsy, you can talk to your mom and William and see what they think. I assume she's staying for the party?"

Maddie dipped her head. "Actually, I never invited her. Once this drama unfolded and then with the suspected murder, it completely slipped my mind. I'd honestly lost hope after last night that we would have a party anytime soon. Maybe it should be a small gathering at the cottage once the crime's solved."

He shrugged. "Whatever works for you. Gran certainly deserves a nice party."

She nodded, still unsure. "So, you really think it's safe even if it turns out that someone's watching Angel?"

"It's probably a coincidence, but I promise to take all precautions on the day. I'm assuming you'll invite most of the town, including the deputies and myself, which will help with that."

"And Steve." Maddie waggled her eyebrows.

Ethan's lips formed a circle. "Detective Jones? How did you manage that?"

"I didn't do a thing. Angel was brought here last night by him and she asked him outright." It gave Maddie a warm glow once more to picture the two of them together.

"I knew he'd done that, but in the time we've known him I've never seen him loosen up much."

Maddie shrugged. "Then, it's going to one heck of a party."

Ethan grinned, then finished his drink. "Right, I'm off to the cottage to see who's awake."

"Gran will be up, and Laura should be here any minute."

"Then I better grab another of these." He kissed her again, reaching behind her back for a fresh doughnut.

"And here I was thinking it was me you couldn't resist."

He kissed her again. "Well, you are as sweet as a doughnut, but man can't live by kisses alone."

A rude sound came from the doorway. Luke stood there with a cheeky grin. "Don't mind me."

Ethan ruffled Big Red's fur and went out laughing, a bite of doughnut the only thing to make him quiet in the stillness of the early morning. He dropped a morsel for Big Red, who gobbled it up before Maddie could tell either of them off.

A loud yawn at the bottom of the stairs signaled Angel's entrance. "Dang if this isn't a noisy place before the birds are even up. Why does Ethan sound so happy?"

Luke reappeared at the door and did a double take, naturally not expecting to see Angel. Certainly not in her pajamas, as decorous as they were. Tousled hair and without makeup, she was still gorgeous, and Maddie shook her head in wonder at the phenomenon as she shared the good news.

"Gran's party is on."

"Wow! That's a big call after last night, isn't it?" Angel was suddenly wide-awake.

"Ethan believes that with most of the force invited, including the detective, we should all be safe enough." Maddie omitted anything about Nicholas, or Ethan's conversation regarding the intruder.

Angel didn't acknowledge the Steve Jones reference. "Cool! Just tell me what you need me to do, and I'm on it."

Glad that Angel seemed to have no ill effects apart from a sore ankle from last night, Maddie pulled out a seat for her and made tea while Luke pulled on his apron and proceeded to check the large whiteboard in the small area designated as Maddie's office. It held the key to each person's duties and what they were baking on any given day.

"There's going to be a lot to do in a short space of time, and we'll need to enlist more volunteers, the sneaky kind, to get Gran out of the way and not let her cotton on to what we're about." Angel helped herself to a doughnut.

"Hopefully with the lack of chat around her birthday, and what with all that's been happening, she won't give it a second thought," Maddie agreed, her mind already racing ahead with ideas she couldn't wait to talk to the Girlz about. Things that would take little amendments to the lists they'd already created.

"Let's catch up tonight," Angel suggested.

Maddie was about to agree when a previous engagement reared its head. "Sorry, I can't. I'm going to Gran's to talk about the funeral on Friday."

Angel's hand shot to her mouth. "Oh, my goodness! It's terrible that the death slips my mind so easily."

Maddie refilled her cup. "Don't worry about it. After all, you never knew Marcus."

"Still, I'd like to be there for you, Gran, Ava, and William. He seems a real sweetie."

Maddie smiled. "He really is. And you know everyone is welcome. Mom might not be so happy about that, but I'm thinking it will be a smaller service than usual for Maple Falls."

Angel nodded. "Then back to Gran's?"

"I think it will have to be the community center."

"You'll have another busy day in the bakery then. Let me know if I can help. I could make eclairs?" Angel offered.

"I appreciate that, but between Gran and me, the food

will be taken care of. Help with serving drinks and taking around platters would be wonderful."

"Consider it done. Let me know the details when you've decided on them so I can move appointments around, and thanks for having me over last night. I must confess I slept like a log."

Maddie grimaced. "I know, I heard you snoring."

Angel snorted. "Impossible."

Luke laughed, until he saw how serious Angel was, then coughed to mask his reaction.

"How is your ankle this morning?" Maddie changed the subject.

Angel stuck a delicate leg out to show a bruise already forming. "Tender, but not so bad, considering how it felt when I turned it."

"That's lucky. Standing all day in the salon would be a nightmare."

Angel grimaced. "That's our jobs for you. I'll get Beth to handle things if it gets too difficult as the day goes on. She's doing so well with hair cutting now that I think she could pass several levels at once. The hard part is convincing her to try."

"Good for her." Maddie was delighted Beth had proven that given a chance the teenager would shine. She was also aware that Luke took particular interest in this conversation. He and Beth were close, and she had no qualms about the girl hearing secondhand how much Angel and Maddie thought of her. They'd already told her several times, but it was nice to have the reinforcement when you doubted your abilities as Beth did.

"Well, I may as well head home and get ready for work. I don't suppose you have another doughnut to send me on my way? I would have eaten an eclair, but we know what happened to them," Angel added with mock horror.

"What happened?" Luke asked.

"Be a dear and grab my bag from upstairs. Maddie can tell you all about it later." Angel smiled.

In all likelihood, Luke would have walked on glass if Angel wanted something, and he was back in a flash with her bag, holding it as if it were made of something precious.

Maddie watched Angel pull on her dressing gown and add a little makeup. It was still early and the roads were empty, but Angel couldn't leave the house unless she looked her best.

Elegant and demure, the expensive pajamas and matching dressing gown could have graced a fashion shoot, and with a few practiced brushes of her hair, Angel sashayed home, barely hobbling at all.

Maddie sighed, automatically tucking a stray lock of hair back into her braid. It had been great having her friend stay. In a way, Angel had helped take Maddie's mind off the troubles, but they were still there. A new day didn't change that.

Chapter Seventeen

T hat afternoon, Maddie headed to the cottage to help with the funeral arrangements for Marcus. Making sure she'd taken care of her tasks, and that Luke and Laura were happy to manage without her, Maddie walked down Plum Place with Big Red.

His presence helped to lighten the dark mood that had come upon her as soon as she'd headed this way. Funerals always brought back memories of her grandad's—the one that naturally touched her family more than any other.

Her mother had been a mess. Angry and more distant than usual, she didn't lift a finger to help. Clearly under no compunction to spend time reminiscing or to sympathize with Maddie and Gran, she'd hidden in her room or elsewhere on the farm. Would she be any different with the loss of Marcus? Maddie assumed not.

Inside the cottage, Ava and William sat at the table holding hands. Maddie swallowed hard. This was a positive sign, even as the sadness on their faces tugged at her heart. Gran gave Maddie a small smile as she brought through a tray of tea things and poured for them all.

"You should have the funeral you think he would like, dear," Gran said to William.

He smiled at Maddie. "We were talking about the format for the funeral. I have absolutely no idea about what I should do. At home the vicar took care of everything." A hitch to his voice was followed by a heavy sigh.

Gran patted his hand. "I spoke to the minister and he said Friday is fine for the funeral as long as the coroner releases Marcus by then. He understood that you don't want to wait too long to take Marcus home. The crematorium is a few hundred yards from the chapel, and the undertaker will take care of the move from one place to the next. They will also get a small booklet printed if you could supply a photo right away. It will tell us a little about him, and it will be nice to see his face."

He nodded. "Thank you. I have one somewhere in my things at the hotel in Destiny."

"You're most welcome, dear. I believe Ethan or Rob will collect your bags today and bring them here." Gran spoke in a soothing voice she used for the sick or scared. Both applied to poor William, who still had a look of shell-shock about him. Although, he did give them a weak smile.

"That is good news. I feel like I've worn these clothes for a week."

"You look fine, dear," Ava told him, sounding very much like Gran.

He kissed Ava's hand. This was still strange to Maddie —to see her mom being affectionate or accepting affection.

Gran was watching them all and must have noticed how the exchange affected Maddie, because she interjected.

"Let's get back to the service. What would you like to happen? Or what do you think Marcus would have wanted?"

"He was a quiet man, but he liked a laugh. He wouldn't want it to be too dark or heavy."

Maddie took notes. "Was he religious?"

William frowned. "He wasn't a churchgoer, but I believe he would like a church service."

Gran nodded. "The minister will be here soon, and he'll have ideas to give poor Marcus a lovely send-off. Do you think he'd like some particular music?"

William brightened. "He adored classical music, like me. The radio was always on wherever he was."

"Suzy can help with that." Maddie volunteered her friend. "She loves all music and has a fantastic collection."

William nodded, while Ava began to fidget. Maddie was reminded again how her mom refused to leave her room when Grandad passed away. They were all devastated, but Ava had been incapable of offering comfort or help with the arrangements. At least William had her by his side, no matter that she looked like she wanted to run.

"Will you do the eulogy?" Gran asked him.

"I'd like to, although it will be rather hard." William sighed heavily, and Ava leaned in closer.

"It's always hard to say goodbye," Ava said softly. "I'll be there to help if it gets too much."

William tucked an arm around his wife and kissed her head in exactly the way Ethan kissed Maddie's. Her heart swelled to see this tenderness. With a man like William at her side, a man she clearly loved, her mom was going to be just fine.

Gran took his other hand. "After the funeral, everyone can come to the community center for tea, if that suits you?"

William's eyes widened. "I hadn't thought about what happens after. Do you think other people will want to come? No one knows me in Maple Falls."

Gran tutted. "That's beside the point. If you would rather come back here, that's fine, or we can go to a hotel in Destiny. There's the resort by the lake too, but people will come to pay their respects and support you. It's just what we do here."

"Mom's right." Ava rolled her eyes. "Even if you wanted to keep it private, it couldn't happen. I imagine there'll be plenty of rubberneckers."

Gran tutted again, and Maddie dropped her pen. Her mom was probably only trying to protect William, but she didn't need to be mean. There was much to be said for a community who stuck by each other even in times of trouble. Sure, the odd person would be there for curiosity, but not the majority. Luckily, William didn't appear perturbed.

"It's okay, my love. If your mum thinks we should go to the community center, then I don't mind. I want Marcus to have a good send-off. It sounds like he would get that there."

"If it's what you really want?" Still dubious that he could, Ava relented.

"Well, I think that's all we need for the moment. Since there isn't any other family around, perhaps it would be better not to have pallbearers?"

He nodded. "That makes sense, and to be honest I don't think I could do it justice. It seems I've turned into a bit of a softie."

"Don't be silly. You're the strongest man I know," Ava retorted and kissed his cheek.

Maddie coughed and stood. "I'll get hold of Ethan and Suzy and get those things sorted. If you don't need me, I'll head home?"

"Of course. We'll be fine." Ava gave her a penetrating look.

As she walked back to the bakery, Maddie let her frustration out to Big Red. "I don't understand how she can be so upset about Marcus and willing to help."

The Maine coon gave her a wise look as he scampered beside her.

"I know she was upset when Grandad passed and was in shock, but we needed her. And for goodness sake, we're family. I suppose Marcus is too, but how long could she have known him for?"

Her cat meowed softly, as if he were telling her to calm down.

She sighed resignedly. "You're right. I guess everyone grieves differently."

She could have sworn that he nodded in agreement, and her steps weren't quite so forceful.

The bakery was closed. Her interns had clean-up under control so Maddie went to make her calls.

Ethan seemed pleased to hear from her. He'd gone to Destiny for the autopsy and picked up William's possessions while he was there. He should be returning soon. Hearing his voice was another balm to the turmoil of her senses, as was the news that Marcus's death was probably an accident.

With Suzy delighted to help with music, Maddie went back downstairs to tell her team about tomorrow's plans. People usually brought a plate of food, but with the potential for so many to turn up, Maddie wanted to make sure there would be plenty.

Luke and Laura didn't hesitate, assuring her that they would do as much as she needed. Then they headed home. Thankful for their understanding, and with Big Red watching her from the doorstep, she decided to give the eclairs another test. Mini ones would be ideal for Friday, and she could take the batch to Gran's later on.

Plus, baking was her go-to when she needed to think. And there was certainly plenty of that to do.

Chapter Eighteen

Friday came around fast.

Unable to sleep, Maddie got up earlier than usual to start food preparations, which included those for the funeral. Big Red was not happy at being woken so early. As far as he was concerned, even the normal 5:00 a.m. was barely decent. Maddie left him on her bed while she showered, giving him time to get his grump over with. Then she made a fuss of him with plenty of hugs plus a small treat by way of apology.

When Laura and Luke arrived at six, she had bread baking and cupcakes ready to ice. Big Red was feeling better about being a baker's cat. The smells fixed most bad moods, but having more of his people around suited him. After a round of petting, he curled up in his downstairs bed just inside Maddie's office, one eye on the proceedings in between naps.

"They look good." Luke nodded at the cupcakes as he put on his apron.

"Thanks. I wanted something that looked nice, yet not too festive."

"Then I won't add sprinkles," Laura said seriously. "Will I start on some slices?"

"Yes, please. I still have the doughnuts for the shop to make, then before lunch I'd like to get the sandwiches done."

"We can do a tag team in the shop if you have anything else you want to bake," Luke offered.

Maddie smiled gratefully at her two interns, who never ceased to amaze her with their dedication and flexibility. "I appreciate that. It's not like you knew Marcus."

"We're happy to help. Now that we've met your mom and William, it does make things more personal. Marcus was part of your new extended family."

When Maddie's smile slipped, Laura got flustered and started the mixer, adding ingredients for the base of a slice, which was a layered dessert cut into squares or rectangles.

Maddie tipped her head. "It does feel odd that I didn't know this man either, and yet today we'll mourn him."

Laura nodded. "Funerals aren't really for the dead, are they?"

"Pardon?" Maddie asked, thinking she'd misheard her.

Laura's cheeks turned pink, but this time she forged ahead. "They're for those left behind. We celebrate their lives and say goodbye. We could do that in so many ways, and yet they're still gone, and how much we love them can never be truly reflected with cake."

Maddie was measuring ingredients for the doughnuts and paused, hand in the air with a scoop of flour. "I had no idea you thought so much about these things."

Laura flushed. "Well, my mother's grandparents were lovely people. Unfortunately, their funeral became about my parents and who they hoped would show up. It was so horribly theatrical, and true mourning, as far as I'm concerned, was nonexistent. I guess that sounds pretty jaded."

Maddie tutted. Poor Laura had it rough in the family stakes, yet it hadn't made her mean the way her parents were. "It's understandable that you'd feel as though a funeral serves no purpose, but it won't be that way today. The people there will be feeding their souls as much as their stomachs as they rally around Ava and William—admittedly, mostly for Gran's sake."

Laura smiled. "You have such a way with words, and I'm sure Maple Falls reacts very differently to a big city funeral."

With time to reflect as they baked, Maddie wondered if Maple Falls was in fact different to other towns.

Ethan came by just as they'd finished the sandwiches. Big Red greeted him at the door with a brutish grab for an ankle. Ethan was too quick and jumped out of the way.

"Whoa, big fella! What's gotten into you? I thought we had a peace treaty."

"Don't mind him, apart from his paws. He's still holding a grudge about our early start this morning, and now you've disturbed his nap. We've also had plenty of people stop by to say they would be coming to the funeral. It's all conspired to stop him from napping, and that's the one thing he can't excuse," Maddie explained, happy to see the handsome sheriff anytime. "I think he should have a time-out."

"He's worse than a child sometimes. Best I keep a wide berth, since I'm the one he's taking it out on." Ethan grinned. "You can smell the baking for miles, so I'm not surprised you've got people coming by already. How's it going?"

"The team have been cooking up a storm, and we're on track to get it done early."

Ethan took off his hat. "I never had a doubt."

She grinned at his conviction. "Why the uniform? I thought you were taking time off?"

"Someone called in sick this morning."

Maddie handed the batter to Luke and moved on to make frosting. "What a shame. I was hoping you could spend the afternoon with us."

Ethan twirled his hat on his finger. "I intend to do both, although looking after William, Ava, and Angel is my priority."

Maddie wasn't sure how to feel about that—disappointed or worried. Maybe both? "Surely there's no need for you to worry about them."

"I'll be with you and the family during the funeral, but you know the case is still open."

Maddie grimaced. If only it weren't. For everyone's sake.

"I have to check in with Detective Jones and my team to make sure enough of us are there today. What time would you like me to come get you?" Ethan asked.

She didn't want to interfere with his job. "I can get there under my own steam."

He stared her down. "What time will you be ready to go?"

Maddie sighed resignedly. "2:00 p.m."

"Then I'll be here, and we can go together in whichever car you choose." He dropped his hat on his head with panache.

The other two stared at her. They knew Maddie was adverse to being told what to do. By anyone.

"I pick my battles. This time I'd quite like him close by," Maddie said before laughing.

Laura's shock eased, and Luke grinned. He definitely got her sense of humor better.

"It's called compromise. A totally different aspect to it when you're talking boyfriends." She winked. "He's bossy, and I'm a control freak. We're working it out—one compromise at a time."

Laura narrowed her gaze thoughtfully as she frosted a slice, and Maddie sorely hoped that her friend was thinking on how to make things work with Deputy Jacobs.

Ethan got back in time to help Luke and Laura load Honey, while Maddie locked up earlier than usual. Then they headed to the community center, where they unloaded the food and refreshments. Mavis, Jed, Nora, and Gran had set the place up already for whoever might show, and Gran's mini apple pies and scones were placed under covers.

With Gran between her friends and Ethan at Maddie's side, they walked the short distance to the church in a small convoy. They were early, but a few people were already there. Luke and Laura chatted to the groups while Maddie and Ethan went inside.

Marcus was already in place under the beautiful stained window in a spectacular casket. Ava stood beside William, who was openly upset. Maddie intended to pat his back, but he turned and hugged her before moving away to wipe his tearstained cheeks.

"Oh dear. I really need to pull myself together." His voice wobbled.

Maddie felt so sorry for his distress. "We understand this is painful for you, and you really don't have to be strong today."

Ava, who disliked emotion, surprised Maddie and Gran when she took his hand and spoke firmly. "Listen to Maddie, Will. It's okay to be sad. No one will think any less of you for grieving this way."

"I can be sad after. It isn't done to be so emotional, even on a day such as this when there's a eulogy to say." With that, he straightened himself and wiped his face on a crumpled handkerchief.

For some reason, his proper English and his fight to stay strong made the day even sadder.

"If you're not up for it, the minister could likely do it for you," Ava suggested.

He shook his head. "Absolutely not. Marcus would be alive if he hadn't been here with me. I owe it to him as a family member and a friend to give him a good send-off. I just wish Nicholas and Amelia could have made it. He's too sick, and his daughter just arrived to take care of him."

"That's a shame, but we're here, and Gran and I will see to the rest of the mourners. You stay inside with Mom and take all the time you need. There's no rush."

"There never is in Maple Falls." Ava's words were said kindly and without her usual rancor.

A tug on Maddie's heart, not for the first time this week, made her aware of how much her mom had changed. William might have brought his troubles to town, but he'd also brought the light into her mother's life, and that was priceless.

"Will you be okay if I go?" Ethan asked casually, searching her face.

He'd changed into a suit and looked so different, but he was the sheriff and he was on duty. She nodded. "You'll still be around?"

"Definitely. I'll be by your side in a heartbeat if you need me."

His assurance helped, but as she watched him leave, she realized that there were no deputies in sight. That was odd. If there was no cause for worry, then they would certainly be part of this gathering. Maddie shook her head. This was not the time to be focusing on mysteries that may or may not be relevant.

Just then a woman came through the doorway and took a seat in the last pew, looking around with interest, yet a little awkward. She was the first mourner to come inside, but Maddie had no idea who she was. Heading over to welcome her, Gran got there first.

"I'd hoped your first Maple Falls get-together would be something other than a funeral, Dinah."

The petite woman in a powder blue jacket and skirt gave a warm smile. "I didn't want to impose, Bea. I went to the community center like you suggested the other day, but no one was there. I found Mavis, who insisted I come. I swear, I didn't know it was a funeral right away, although the dark clothes should have been a clue. To be honest, I was hoping for a wedding or christening."

Gran gave a short laugh at the woman's surprise at where she'd ended up. "That's Mavis's charm, and you are most welcome. Many of the people coming today don't know my son-in-law and certainly not his cousin, the deceased."

The woman was contrite. "I'm sorry for your loss."

"Thank you. This is my granddaughter, Madeline Flynn."

Something about the woman's open face drew Maddie to her. "Everyone calls me Maddie."

"I'm Dinah Dolomore. I hear from Mavis and Nora that your bakery is wonderful."

"Please stop by and try a free sample."

She grinned. "I'll be sure to. Now that I'm unpacked, I feel like I can breathe again."

"Moving's not fun, is it?"

"Not at all, but I suspect this will be my last one." Dinah winked at them.

Just then the sound of voices became louder, and people began to enter the church. Most of them were Gran's friends from the community center and retirement village, but others had come from all over town and, as always happened, there were a few rubberneckers.

"Please excuse us."

Gran took hold of Maddie's arm, and they left the friendly woman to her new friend. Mavis would certainly look after her.

Suzy, Angel, and Laura handed out the booklets that the funeral director had printed in a hurry. The picture on the front was of a round-faced man with similar features to William and the same thick dark hair with some sprinkles of silver. It was a nice face, Maddie decided. Much nicer than when she'd seen him in the woods. She shivered as she remembered that pointing finger once more.

William managed the eulogy and only cried when the coffin was taken to the crematorium. He walked behind the hearse the few hundred yards with head bowed. Determined to say one last goodbye in private, he looked so bereft that Ava decided to catch up to him, but Gran took her arm.

"Let him be, child. He has some grieving to do that will help him come to terms with this. You fix your face and be here when he returns to help him then."

Ava nodded and meekly went to the bathroom. Maddie

shook her head at the unlikely scenario but had no time to dwell on it when Gran's friends came to chat, along with the Girlz.

"Such a lovely service," Mavis gushed.

"They're not meant to be lovely," Nora intoned.

Mavis shook her head. "Rubbish. The nicer a funeral, the nicer the person. Everybody knows that."

Nora snorted, and Gran winked at Maddie.

"Will we head back to the community center and get the drinks underway, sugar?" Angel interrupted, a smile playing with her mouth.

"That would be lovely. Gran and I will wait for Mom and William, but it would be unfair to make everyone else mill around when we don't know how long we'll be," Maddie said.

"Mavis and Nora will give you a hand, Angel. Won't you?" Gran prompted.

Mavis was a little discombobulated at being asked in so many words to leave, however she loved to help, so there was no fuss. With that settled and the crowd encouraged to head to the center, by the time Ava emerged, fresh as a daisy, the area was almost empty. A couple of chatting stragglers got the idea, and soon they were alone.

To break the silence, Maddie told Gran and her mom what Laura had said about funerals, and Gran nodded.

"If you think about what we know happens at funerals, it's true. The deceased is gone and hopefully headed for a better place."

Ava gave Gran a long look. "I didn't think you were particularly religious."

"Just because a person isn't in church every week has nothing to do with belief, child. Being the best a person can be is what matters."

Ava clasped her hands together and sighed deeply. "I'm sorry I wasn't the perfect child you deserved, Mom."

Gran let out a breath on a whoosh. "I never wanted a perfect child."

"One that wasn't so much trouble would have been better than me." Ava grinned ruefully.

"I can't deny that less trouble has its appeal, but I loved and still love you, because *you* are my daughter, not some fictional one you think I wanted. I just wanted a child who was happy."

They sat staring into each other's eyes, one set oddly unsure, the other surrounded by small crinkles, and yet the blue so vibrant in each.

Maddie's heart felt full. This was a moment that should be etched in time, so that whenever they disagreed in the future—a likelihood that couldn't be denied—they could pull out this memory and show each other that love wasn't something easily discarded. Sometimes a person had to be willing to forgive more times than they cared to, but it could be worth it if you gave it one more chance. The way Gran always did.

William appeared along the end of the small road, head bowed once more. As he got closer, his shoulders straightened, and by the time he got to the silent group, he managed a watery smile.

"Marcus will be ready for pickup in a couple of days," he told them, looking steadily across the green grass of the churchyard.

Gran stood. "Then we can't do more today. Let's go have some tea with our friends."

Ava grimaced, but hand-in-hand, she and William followed them down the road to the community center.

Chapter Nineteen

The center was buzzing. All the regulars sat in their usual spots, Gran's chair left vacant, and the new lady sat in between Mavis and Nora.

Jed leaped to his feet and organized a cup of tea for Gran while Angel and Suzy brought out cups for Maddie, Ava, and William, whose hands shook slightly as he acknowledged everyone who spoke to him. He even managed a smile or two.

Ava hung back, but not too far from William. Looking like a bird seeking an escape, when her eyes lighted on Maddie she shrugged in reply to Maddie's mouthed, "Are you okay?" Ava might grow more comfortable one day, but this was not that day.

Bursting with excitement and at the same time trying to appear somber, Mavis couldn't help asking anyone who came near, "Have you met Dinah?"

It was Maddie's turn. "I have. Welcome again to Maple Falls."

Dinah seemed perfectly comfortable between the

mismatched pair. "Thank you, dear. Everyone has been so friendly. I wish I'd made the move years ago."

"She's moved into the apartment next to mine. Isn't that wonderful? We have so much in common," Mavis gushed.

"Not for her," Nora said. "The woman will be lucky to get a word in edgewise."

Mavis gave a merry tinkle. "You're such a tease, Nora."

Nora glared, but Dinah wasn't put off at all.

"These two are so much fun. I have a feeling I'm going to be happy here."

"I hope you are. If you have any problems, you let me know," Gran said with a sideways glance to Nora, who primly looked the other way.

Maddie smothered a laugh and went to fetch some plates of food.

"Have you spoken to your mom about the party?" Angel whispered when they were alone for a moment in the large kitchen.

Maddie looked around her to ensure it was indeed just the two of them. "Not yet. It hasn't felt appropriate."

"I know, sugar, but they'll head to London soon. If you don't tell them, they won't have the opportunity to stay. I might be way off, but you all seem to be getting on better than I've ever seen."

Maddie couldn't argue. "I'll do it as soon as I can get them away from everyone and Gran's not near."

"Good plan. While it's a shame for poor Marcus, at least Gran hasn't had a whiff of any of our plans."

Maddie grimaced. "I wouldn't put money on that. To be honest, I haven't been thinking about it at all. Luckily the mayor penciled us in when I first spoke to her about hiring the building and area they use for festivals and market day at Maple Fields. It turns out that the large tent will be up already for the spring festival the following week, so we can use it for the party."

Angel gasped. "Wow! That's a fantastic start. The invites are going out tomorrow, via word of mouth. If we don't reach everyone, so be it."

Just then Nora came into the kitchen. "Are you bringing those plates anytime soon, or shall I take them?"

"Sorry, Nora. They're coming now, but there are more if you'd like to help?" Maddie knew the woman's bark was worse than her bite and that she was kind underneath her rough exterior, and Nora proved this.

"I'll help for Gran's party too, if it's still on?"

Maddie hesitated. "Oh. It's still a surprise."

"You don't think I can keep my mouth shut? I'm not Mavis, you know."

"Of course I didn't think that. We were just talking about it, and your help would be wonderful. We'll be in touch tomorrow, if that's okay?" Maddie lowered her voice as they neared the main room.

"It's not as if I'm knee-deep in activity." Nora sniffed and followed them out with a plate in each hand.

Angel walked ahead of them, her shoulders shaking as she hid her laughter from Nora.

"She's such a pretty girl, isn't she, dear?" Dinah said to Maddie while helping herself to a sandwich.

"Angel? She is, with a personality to fit."

"You girls are close, I understand."

"Suzy, Angel, Laura, and I are the best of friends. We're with each other so often everyone calls us the Girlz." Maddie smiled.

"Yes, I heard that. It's like a new generation following in Mavis, Gran, and Nora's footsteps."

Maddie tilted her head. "I suppose it is. Although you'd have to include Jed in that group."

"Your Gran's boyfriend?"

Maddie almost dropped her plates. "They're just friends."

"Really? I thought. . . Oh, don't mind me. I'm a silly old woman who talks too much." Dinah's cheeks flushed.

They were interrupted by Mavis, who was desperate to try a brownie off the other plate Maddie held, even though she'd had one a week since Maddie's shop opened a year ago.

Maddie smiled at them and moved on, a little dazed by Dinah's words. Gran and Jed were close, and it wasn't as if she hadn't thought about the two of them as more than friends, but Gran never indicated it was more. Jed, on the other hand, had several times done so in throwaway comments.

How would she feel about it being true? Why, it wouldn't be the worst thing. She loved Gran and wanted her to be happy, and never had a cross word with Jed. He was a gentleman in every way and cared very much about Gran's welfare.

With that foremost in her mind, it was another prompt to tell Ava about the party. The time wasn't as good as it could be—or was it? Ava seemed to be more receptive to Gran, and if Maddie told her how much it would mean, surly she would want to stay?

The opportunity didn't present itself, because after William thanked them all for coming, he and Ava decided to walk home. It would take some time, and Maddie guessed they wanted to talk privately. She was disappointed yet relieved.

The Girlz and Gran's friends would clean up the

community center, and this time Maddie didn't resent her mom for not helping.

Ethan hung around the periphery for the time they were there, eventually disappearing outside. She wasn't sure where he'd be now, but her feet were complaining about the hours spent on them.

"I'll take all the dishes back to the bakery, if you are all okay to finish up here?"

"Of course, dear." Gran waved her away. "Jed's offered to take me home."

That made Maddie thoughtful again as Luke helped her load Honey. When she arrived at her garage, she saw a couple across the road at the park under the large Maple tree. Ava and William. She parked Honey and decided on the spur of the moment to broach the subject of the party while she had them alone.

"Sorry to interrupt," she called as she got closer.

"We're just having some quiet time," Ava said gently.

"Thank you for organizing today and making all the food," William added. "You did Marcus proud."

"I'm so glad you think so." Maddie smiled, then began to tap her thigh.

"Is everything okay?" Ava looked pointedly at her fingers.

"I have something to tell you, and I appreciate that now is not the best time, but I know you have plans to leave in a couple of days."

Ava grimaced. "This doesn't sound good."

"No, it's fine, and whatever you decide won't change anything but I wanted you to know."

"Good grief, you sound like Mavis. Get to the point, would you?" Her mom's impatience won out.

William patted Ava's leg. "Let the girl speak, dear."

Maddie smiled her thanks. "It's Gran's seventieth birthday Saturday week. I'm organizing a large party at Maple Fields. I'd like you both to be there, but I understand if that's not possible."

"We're leaving in a couple of days." Ava looked to William.

He shook his head firmly. "Of course we'd love to stay."

Ava gasped. "But what about Marcus?"

"I think he'd understand. Besides, it won't matter to him whether he's here for a few more days or in the family crypt in Devon," William said solemnly.

"I guess not." Ava shrugged. "I guess we'll stay."

Maddie's heart did a flip. "That's wonderful news. It is a surprise, so it would be great if you could formulate an excuse for staying that wouldn't sound suspicious to Gran."

"You mean lie? I think I can manage that." Ava raised an eyebrow, but her tone was definitely teasing.

Maddie smiled at her mom, unsure if Ava was truly happy to stay in Maple Falls for any reason or was simply wanting to please William. Then she decided it didn't matter, because Gran was going to have the best birthday ever.

Chapter Twenty

The next week was taken up with people dropping by the bakery to ask about the party. With the town sworn to secrecy, Maddie worried every second that someone would let slip the plans.

Ava and William proved to be brilliant allies and were keeping Gran entertained by getting her to show William around town and the countryside. In Maddie's eyes, the man deserved a medal!

The Monday cooking class was going well, with her students making a huge effort so they could contribute to the table at the birthday with a new recipe—ginger biscuits.

The men were improving and taking things more seriously. In fact, there was talk of a competition between them. As they loaded the trays into the cabinet oven, Maddie could see that their biscuits were uniform and looked a good consistency.

Mavis giddily clapped her hands in delight when the door closed on them. She'd been looking likely to explode any minute, and Maddie suspected it was around all the secrecy of the party. Hopefully, Gran was too busy to spend much time with her, and Mavis seemed to be taken with her new neighbor.

"Dinah Dolomore is a wonderful cook, isn't she, Nora?"

Nora shrugged while wiping down her portion of the counter. "Pretty good."

"Oh, you! That curry she cooked us last night was divine."

"I'm not much of a curry person." Nora screwed up her face.

Mavis elbowed her, sending small bits of batter from her fingers over the clean space. "Then why would you have two helpings?"

"Your biscuits are burning," Nora told her, wiping the surface.

"No!" Mavis shot across the room as though she'd been fired from a cannon.

Maddie tutted as the rest of the group followed Mavis to check on their prized efforts. "Nora, that's not kind. I just checked, and all the biscuits are doing just fine."

"My mistake," Nora said, straight-faced, but a twinkle in her eye told a different story.

Maddie didn't pursue it. "Nora, I need you to get Gran to the party at 3:30 p.m. precisely on Friday."

"Why me?" Genuinely shocked, Nora exploded.

Maddie lowered her voice. "Because you won't give the game away and you'll make sure everyone's on time."

The older woman preened a little. "I'll get Jed to bring us."

"Good. Now we need a pretense."

"I'll say that we need to look at the new rotunda at the resort. Mavis has been talking about it for ages, and it's on the way. That should appease Gran, since she's mentioned it once or twice."

Relieved, Maddie was in danger of hugging her. "I knew you were the right choice."

"Okay. Don't overdo it." Nora laughed, taking a step back.

The sight was such a rare occurrence that Maddie didn't know what to say. With a raised eyebrow and lingering self-satisfied smile, Nora headed to the oven.

Chapter Twenty-One

T he day of the party dawned as a particularly beautiful spring day. The view from Maddie's bedroom showed spring flowers blooming not only in her garden but across the road in the park. Underneath the massive maple tree, daffodils waved in a gentle breeze. Maddie sighed happily as she and Big Red went downstairs.

Jed had been charged with taking Gran to Destiny yesterday, meaning that the baking could begin in earnest.

Nora had asked Gran to stop by today and help her with her knitting, which would hopefully prevent Gran from turning up, since Nora never asked for help. Maddie had said business was slow as another deterrent.

Cakes, slices, and pies were now packaged for the trip to Maple Fields. Cupcakes awaiting their frosting sat in boxes in the walk-in chiller, along with mini eclairs. This morning was all about bacon and egg pies, quiches, and sandwiches added to the usual baking for a Saturday.

Luke looked after the shop while Laura, Suzy, and

Maddie made delicate club sandwiches. Three layers of bread with fillings like egg, lettuce, tomato, or ham, cheese, and pickle took time and patience, but Maddie knew they were worth the effort.

"Mine aren't looking as nice as yours," Suzy noted with a frown.

"They look fine. Besides, trust me, no one will notice how they look once they start on the food."

Suzy laughed. "Having seen the townsfolk in action, you might be right."

"What time will Gran arrive at Maple Fields?" Laura asked.

"Jed's going to stop by Nora's and explain that it was such a lovely day he figured they should take a drive out to the resort to see the new rotunda and have some afternoon tea for 3:00 p.m."

"Good plan. What time will we need to take the food?"

"Bernie and Chris Jamieson are coming here with their car and van. I'll take the last in Honey and close up about two."

"Do you think you'll get any complaints about closing early?" Laura wondered.

Maddie snorted. "When most of the town is coming, I don't think there will be too many."

"I wonder if Gran suspects anything?" Luke asked as he piped cream into eclairs between serving customers.

Maddie shrugged. "I hope not, but she could just be playing along. Actually, I'm okay with that. When she sees everyone, I think she'll be pleased. Even though being the center of attention isn't her favorite thing."

Luke nodded. "Without making things depressing, I'm so glad everything was resolved enough to carry on with the party."

"Me too. Gran deserves to see how much she's loved in Maple Falls." Maddie said.

Suzy nodded. "She's helped nearly every single person here in one way or another."

This talk made Maddie a little misty. Gran was just Gran to her, but she really was so much more. President of the community center, catalyst for the gray brigade at the country club being more tolerant of those less fortunate, a stalwart of child and animal rights, and a pillar of the community in general.

No matter how she tried, Maddie could never say enough about the woman who raised her. She hoped when it came time for speeches, others charged with doing so would do Gran justice.

Bernie and Chris bounded up the steps on cue. Maple Falls would be looking like a ghost town right now, with most of the shops shut, but Gran wouldn't notice if she stayed where she was.

"Luke, could you help load the vehicles, please? I'll watch the shop."

"I'll help too." Laura began to take off her apron.

"No need." Deputy Jacobs came through the door. "I'd like to help."

Out of uniform, he looked younger, with a sweet self-consciousness about him when he was near Laura. Her intern awkwardly put her apron back on, face suffused with color, patting her hair, which was in its usual red bun.

Maddie put the last of the sandwiches in a box. "Thank you, Rob. Another vehicle is a bonus too. When you're loaded, it would make sense for you to go with Rob, Laura. You'll be able to get some of the setup done before I get there."

Rob and Laura looked at each other, both pink-cheeked.

Maddie could see that Rob was looking forward to spending time with Laura again, and her friend didn't protest. Laura wasn't playing hard to get, she was simply scared of letting Rob get any closer. Today it seemed that she was less agitated about that.

Maddie totally appreciated her dilemma, having fought against the attraction to Ethan. The difference was Maddie had known Ethan most of her life and they had been boyfriend and girlfriend for many years as teenagers. Laura once mentioned that she'd never had a boyfriend, and the rest of the Girlz imagined it would be rather terrifying to be in their late twenties with no experience of men.

Solving crimes might be something Maddie inherited from her grandad, but her matchmaking genes came purely from Gran. She wanted her friends to find happiness just as she had, and in her not so humble opinion, Laura and Rob were ideal for each other.

"If that's what you need?" Laura removed her apron, smoothing down a gorgeous green dress she'd snuck out of the cottage last week and left in Maddie's bedroom.

"Yes, thanks." Maddie noticed how Rob's eyes widened, then remained on Laura the whole time she organized his load.

With the vehicles full, the others set off. Luke and Maddie gathered serving platters, frosting, piping bags and other necessities, plus the cake. Then they locked up and headed out to Honey.

Big Red sat beside the rear door, and Maddie stopped dead. She hadn't thought to take him. Did cats belong at a party miles from home? But he was family. She opened the door, and he jumped in, giving the full back seat a grumpy glance.

"It's the floor or stay behind," she told him.

He fluffed himself into a ball and curled up behind the driver seat, much to Luke's amusement.

"He really does understand you."

"I suspect far more than he lets on as well." Maddie shut the door with a laugh.

Driving slowly, worried for her full car, Maddie concentrated on missing any potholes, while Luke held firmly to the cake. It was a giant teacup and saucer done as Gran's real set. Lilacs adorned the rim of the saucer, and on top sat a fondant rolling pin, an 70th flag stuck in the middle of it. *Happy Birthday Gran* was written across the front of the cake in delicate petals in a variety of colors. Maddie couldn't be prouder of a cake she'd made and knew Gran would love it.

When they got to Maple Fields at two thirty, the car park was already filling. Maddie had a space reserved for her, which made things easier. Together she and Luke took the cake to the area that had been set up for the food under the tent. A single round table covered in lacework donated by Mavis stood front and center, and carefully they positioned the cake to face the room.

Behind this were several trestle tables, already groaning with the food her team had prepared, plus other plates from the townspeople. The result was more gorgeous food than she could imagine being eaten in a couple of days, but as more and more people arrived, her opinion on that changed dramatically.

At 3:00 p.m., everything was done. Stragglers continued to arrive, but most people had found a place to sit and were taking constant note of the time, just as Maddie was.

Ethan entered the area, followed by Ava and William.

Ava was stunning in a blue trouser suit with gold shot through the jacket, while William wore his standard black suit. Ethan, resplendent in his dress uniform and looking more handsome than ever, waved to her.

Maddie was relatively convinced the thudding of her heart was caused by seeing him come toward her. Although, having her mom at a family occasion was such a major thing, so she couldn't be sure.

"You've done an amazing job," Ava said, holding on to William with a white-knuckled grip. "I wish I could have contributed."

"Gran would have suspected something if you'd been at the bakery, and we have plenty." Maddie waved at the food. "It was a team effort with lots of other people helping too. I'm just glad you're here." Maddie added this awkwardly, because she wanted to say so much more, but didn't know how.

Her mom gave her a wry smile without relaxing her grip.

William smiled at them. "It looks wonderful. Your gran can only be delighted by this show of affection. Now, where should we sit?"

"We have a family table in front of the cake," Maddie interjected before Ava could steer him to the back of the tent as she surely would prefer. "The big comfy chair is for Gran. Perhaps you could sit one side of her and I could sit the other?" she suggested.

"Really? Couldn't I sit somewhere less . . .?"

William pulled her close. "Ava, we talked about this. It's just a few hours. I'm right beside you, and so are Maddie and her friends."

"But they don't want me here," Ava said, so softly Maddie almost missed it.

"Who? The townsfolk?" Maddie asked.

Ava nodded.

"You're not here for them, dear. Your mother should have your support today." William adopted a no-nonsense tone that magically made a difference.

Ava straightened her back and allowed him to lead her to the table. Maddie, while grateful to William, was sorry that her mother couldn't let her past go enough to enjoy the now.

Angel had enlisted the Girlz to man a refreshment counter with fruit punch, bottles of grape juice, and beer. Champagne sat waiting to be opened when Gran arrived, and Maddie felt the bubbles of excitement swirling around her. If she wasn't careful, she'd wind up as giddy as Mavis.

"The decorations are awesome, Angel."

Angel grinned. "Thanks. I had plenty of help from Ethan's sister Layla. Plus her twins, and Noah and Beth. It's been fun."

When no amount of searching could find one tent large enough for so many people, they settled on opening the back so everyone could see Gran and feel a part of the event, hoping it wouldn't rain.

Pots of purple irises decorated the entrance at the front of the tent, which Gran would be brought through. Each table had a round glass bowl with a different colored flower floating in shallow water. Fairy lights dangled over the roof and down the poles, and almost everyone commented on how beautiful the place looked.

With minutes until Gran arrived, Maddie made sure all the final touches were in place. She was close to the front of the tent when Big Red made a run for the opening, and Maddie grabbed him just as she heard a car drive up. Turning to the crowd, she waved furiously. The motion was seen by her crew, and in a few seconds, everyone stood and was impressively quiet. Even the children seemed to appreciate the moment.

A hand came into the tent on one side of the opening, and then one on the other side. They pushed the flaps back simultaneously as far as they could go.

"I'm sure it doesn't need all of us to check the tent is ready for the festival next week," Gran said as she stepped inside ahead of Mavis, Nora, and Jed.

"Surprise!" hundreds of people yelled.

Gran's mouth dropped open, and her handbag fell from her hand. Maddie wanted to pump the air. No one could fake that level of surprise. Not even Gran. They'd achieved the impossible.

"Oh, my!" Gran held her hands to her cheeks. "What's this all about?"

While Nora picked up her bag, Jed pointed to their fellow community center attendees, who launched into an exuberant rendition of "Happy Birthday," whereby the rest of the crowd joined in. It was slightly off-key and very loud. And absolutely amazing.

Tears trailed down Gran's cheeks as Maddie led her to the cake.

"This is stunning!"

"I learned from the best," Maddie assured her.

"It's better than anything I could do." Gran kissed her cheek before smiling out into the room. "There are so many people. How on earth did you keep this a secret, you terrible, wonderful child?"

Maddie laughed, a little choked up as Gran kissed her again. "We all made this happen." Her arms spread to the whole group. "The town loves you."

Gran wept openly. From beside them came a sob. They turned to find Ava in William's arms. Gran wiped her face on the handkerchief she kept in her purse and went to her daughter, pulling her from William. They cried as one, and now Maddie was a mess.

"You stayed for my birthday?" Gran suddenly asked as if it were critical.

"Why else?" Ava sniffed.

"Is this a party or a funeral?" Nora demanded.

Maddie was shocked, but a few titters sounded around the group and pulled smiles from Gran and Ava. In a short time, it seemed as though everyone was laughing again.

Gran whispered in Ava's ear, and the two of them came to Maddie where she stood sniffing by the cake.

"As sad as it is to destroy something so beautiful, and as long as you have a picture of it, I want both of you to help me cut this cake," Gran said.

The three generations held the knife, hands on top of each other's as Gran sliced through the cup into the saucer part of the cake. A cheer resounded around the space. Maddie's happiness scale was all but broken, and she didn't know whether to laugh or cry.

"We should go thank our friends and the community for coming," Gran suggested.

"I'm going to clean myself up," Ava said, already backing away.

Maddie appreciated this might be a step too far for her mom, so she and Gran began the mammoth task while the rest of the Girlz and some helpers, including Mavis and Nora, made tea and coffee.

She'd spied Ethan earlier at the back of the tent and several more times as she and Gran made the rounds. She hoped he would come find her soon, and thinking about that made her realize that she hadn't seen her mom or William in a while.

Then a bloodcurdling scream sounded from the parking area out the front.

Chapter Twenty-Two

Maddie raced to the entrance. The flaps had been closed after everyone arrived, and she ripped open the fastening as quickly as she could. The ablution block edged the left side of the smaller carpark, and she could see her mother's fair head bent over William's dark one.

Running across the open ground, she heard footsteps behind her, and by the time she reached her mom, she was flanked by Deputy Jacobs and a large man with brown hair.

Ava pointed toward the road. "Nicholas," she sobbed. "He tried to get William into his car, and when he couldn't he knocked him out."

With only a little dust in the air and the sound of squealing tires, Nicholas was gone, but from the main carpark an unmarked blue sedan gave chase. Ethan!

Maddie pulled her phone from her pocket and called an ambulance while checking William's pulse. It was thready, and blood trickled from his nose.

"Will he be okay?" Ava's voice came out strangled.

"I'm sure he will. He's a strong man," Maddie told her in between giving details.

A man burst through the throng.

"Where were you?" Ava glared at Jerry.

"Sorry, Ava. I was doing a check around the perimeter when this happened. The sheriff received a call from his deputy and while he gave chase, he told me to relay the message we should get back to the cottage when Mr. Blackwell is okay."

Ava sniffed.

"Tell us what happened, mom."

"When I came out of the bathroom, they were down the driveway. I never even heard a car arrive. Nicholas was so angry and upset about being poisoned. He wanted to get William away from here. Away from me!" She held her husband's hand, kissing the back of it. "He raved about having the funeral without him, but I know for a fact that William tried to reach him several times. The way he spoke made it sound as though William was crazy for wanting to stay. When William wouldn't listen and kept walking away, it just made Nicholas angrier. He pulled on William's arm, and that's when William shoved him. Nicholas hauled back and punched him right in the face."

Ava dabbed at William's face with the sleeve of her dress. "I wasn't wrong about his hatred for me. It's still in his eyes." Through her tears, Ava seemed confused. "But he sounded so frightened, and when he saw the blood he looked horrified."

Her mom's rambling words began to sink in.

"So, you think we've been wrong about him?" Maddie was annoyed and frustrated, and it came out in her voice.

Ava's lips trembled.

Having done the unthinkable by accepting her mother's take on the situation, Maddie had made a cardinal mistake. Studying the flaccid features of her stepfather—it still gave her a jolt to think of him this way—she realized that she should have paid more attention to William's viewpoint.

After all, William had grown up with and knew Nicholas best. Mom had only known the brother for a short time, and they hadn't gotten on. Since there were many people who felt the same about Ava, it stood to reason that her opinion might be flawed.

William had proven to be loving and loyal to both Ava and his brother. He was gentle and kind, and Maddie wanted so much for him to be okay.

"I don't know what to think. This is all too much." Ava began to weep.

Maddie squeezed her mom's shoulder. Being angry at her wouldn't help the fact that there were so many unanswered questions. The main one being, who killed Marcus if it wasn't Nicholas? It appeared that they were right back at the beginning.

The crowd was kept back by Bernie, Chris, and Noah, but Gran and the Girlz edged closer, with, Mavis, Jed, and Nora behind them. Angel handed Ava tissues, and Suzy folded her sweater to place under William's head. Laura brought water and a towel to press to the wound.

Maddie smiled her thanks, but was focused on something that nagged at her. Marcus. "Love can take many forms. Not all of them are healthy."

Ava looked up, giving Maddie a wary look through her tears.

"I mean the brothers with their cousin," Maddie clarified. "Not us."

"William told me how close all three of them were as

children. It would be hard to let that go, even over a disagreement, wouldn't it?" Ava's voice trembled.

Maddie nodded. "That's what I'm thinking." She had no siblings, but Suzy and Angel had taken up the mantle, and when Maddie went to New York she'd missed them terribly and insisted on them visiting every chance they could.

Conversation ceased with the ambulance's arrival. Mitchell Drummond, the paramedic lugging a large bag, knelt beside William, checking his pulse, then lifting his eyelids to shine a penlight on the pupils.

William blinked, then he was staring at them in confusion.

"Lie still, Mr. Blackwell," Mitch told him.

"Why? I'm fine." He sat up despite the paramedic's hands holding him down. "Where's Nicholas?"

"He ran off," Ava told him with a sniff.

"Ethan will find him." Maddie wiped blood off his shirt.

William grabbed her hand. "He won't arrest him, surely?"

"Not if you don't press charges."

"I won't." William shook his head, wincing.

Mitch checked him over again. "The bleeding's stopped. If you feel okay, let's get you to your feet."

William obliged with Mitch and Maddie's help, and then Ava was in between them holding William's cheeks. "You had me so worried."

William smiled wanly. "I'm fine, dear." He turned to face the family and guests lined up around them. "I'm so sorry this is ruining the day."

"Shush," Gran said. "It's not your fault."

"But we know how much time Maddie and the Girlz spent on this," Ava said miserably.

Maddie shook her head. "Don't think about that. Just take care of each other."

Ava did something so out of character, Maddie could only stand in shock. Her mom kissed her cheek, followed by a hug, and did the same to Gran. "Happy birthday, Mom."

Gran's laugh came with a hitch. "Goodness. My heart is jumping all over the place."

Maddie gulped. "Mine too."

Their arms around each other, they turned back to the guests.

"I guess we need to send people home?" Gran said, practical as ever.

"No, let them finish up. If someone else is out there, we should be the ones to go, like Ethan said."

"I never wanted a fuss, anyway. Just being with my family is good enough," Gran was emphatic. "You stay with your mom and William, Maddie. I'll get the team onto this."

"The Girlz will help." Maddie called them over and told them her plan, while Gran went to speak to Jed, Mavis, and Nora.

"Don't you worry, sugar. We'll get them fed and watered and clean up here," Angel said. "You take the family home."

"Please make sure everyone gets a slice of cake too."

"I'll do that," Luke offered.

Maddie sighed with relief that the incident hadn't happened earlier. Gran had at least enjoyed part of her birthday, and the three generations had been given several moments that they might all cherish.

All that was left was to find the murderer. Piece of cake.

As the guests ate, Noah played soothing music, and Maddie headed out to the car with her family, including Big Red, who appeared to have eaten a great deal already.

Rob stood by Honey.

"You've been here the whole time?" Maddie asked.

"I saw what happened, but was too far away to help. After Ethan called, Detective Jones and I stayed behind with another two deputies. I'll escort you home and bring Jerry."

Maddie heard something in his voice despite his impassive face. Something was up. Should she tell him her plan?

"I don't want my brother arrested," William said firmly.

"That's not my call, sir." Rob moved back so they could get in the car.

"Can I talk to you when we get to the house, Deputy Jacobs?" Maddie asked.

That raised his eyebrows. "I'll see you there."

His answer had a justifiable wariness. Sharing his information might not happen, but she had to tell him what she was thinking. Ethan wouldn't be happy if she went off on her own.

Chapter Twenty-Three

Maddie drove carefully, hearing Ava and William's voices but not listening. Somehow she had to follow her instinct and not upset her family.

"What are you up to?" Gran asked softly.

"What do you mean?"

Gran sighed. "Really? You're going to play that game?"

"It's not a game, and it may be nothing. I need to go to the park where Marcus was found."

"It's something dangerous if you're going by yourself." Gran crossed her arms.

"I'm going to ask Rob to come with me."

"Why don't you simply tell him what you mean to do?"

She knew Gran was worried but Maddie was sure she was right. "I have a hunch that I need to look into. Myself."

Gran sighed again and looked out the window. "Don't you go spoiling my birthday by getting yourself hurt."

Maddie smiled. "I wouldn't dream of it."

Gran reached across the seat and squeezed Maddie's leg.

They didn't need to say more, but Maddie loved the familiar warmth that crept through her.

When they got to the cottage, Ava and William went inside. Gran hovered at the door for a moment to blow Maddie a kiss, before following them.

"Oh, boy. This is worse than I'd anticipated," Rob said.

He'd parked his car behind Honey and wore a frown so deep Maddie almost laughed.

"It's not so bad," she told him with a straight face.

"I thought you were wanting to pump me for information, but you're up to something, right?"

He had every right to say this, since they had worked on a few cases by now, but she needed to be gentle with him, otherwise he might stop her from going. "So you do have information?"

"Maybe. You first."

Maddie nodded. "When we found Marcus, he was pointing."

"I remember." Rob shivered.

"What was he pointing at?"

He shrugged. "Who knows? We checked the area."

"I know you did, and I'm sure you all did a fantastic job. The thing is, there wasn't much blood where he was found."

"And?"

"So he was moved there."

"I'm sure that's not your point. Go on."

Maddie raised her hands. "Where was he moved from?"

"You don't think we looked into that? We don't know. The ground was flattened a little along the line we entered the woods. That's all." Frustration had crept into Rob's tone, and Maddie was afraid she'd pushed him too far.

"It's just a hunch, but I want to go back to the woods and look somewhere else."

"No way. Ethan would kill me."

Maddie shrugged. "Naturally he would take me if he was here, but he's off after Nicholas, and I don't know how long he'll be. I honestly think we have to do this now. Someone killed Marcus, and we're no closer to finding that person."

"Ethan will catch Mr. Blackwell."

Maddie shook her head. "But none of us believe it's him. Even Mom is doubtful."

"Nevertheless, it's too dangerous for you to go to the woods."

Maddie crossed her arms. "But how can it be if you're assuming Nicholas is the killer? Besides, you can take me. I'm sure the detective is around somewhere."

That stopped Rob for a moment. Then he tilted his head. "If I don't take you, you'll go anyway. Won't you?"

Maddie shrugged.

Rob sighed heavily. "Let me check the house once more. Wait here."

Maddie took the time to change into some old shoes she kept in the back. Her dress wasn't right for a trip to the woods, but she didn't want to go home and change.

Rob came back and made a call, then he nodded to her. "Let's go on your wild goose chase."

"Yes, Deputy," she said as meekly as she could.

Rob sighed again, and they walked down Plum Place.

"It's your turn. What's your information?" she asked conversationally, wondering if this was a stupid idea. She could be at the cottage spending time with Gran, and her mom who was leaving soon. Just when they were making inroads to a less fractious relationship. Hopefully.

"Really? You asked questions and told me nothing," Rob scoffed.

Maddie made a rude sound, but they became quiet as they crossed the park and headed into the woods. A yellow tape was still in place around the area where Marcus was found.

"We can't go in there," Rob told her.

"I don't want to." She took him by the shoulders and stood him in front of the tape, facing her.

He was naturally perturbed by the manhandling. "What are you doing?"

"Sorry. I'm using you as a marker. Marcus pointed this way."

Rob frowned. "He was dead, and as you suggested, probably moved. The finger could be pointing in any direction."

"Maybe. But what if he wasn't quite dead when he was put behind the log? The fact that his arm was under a branch and yet stuck out beneath it has bugged me since that first day."

He raised an eyebrow. "You never mentioned it."

Maddie shrugged. "It bugged me, but I couldn't figure out why until today."

"Okay, I'll play along. What now?"

He sounded more intrigued now, so Maddie turned away from him but walked in a line from where he stood. It led her to the boulder. Many branches covered one side of it, and Maddie pushed some aside. A black line ran from a sharp piece of stone.

"Rob!" she called.

He was beside her in a heartbeat. "Well done. If I'm not mistaken, that's blood."

"I think so too. It's so little and look at the swipe marks. Someone' tried to clean it and cover it up. But look what's attached to it." She pointed to several strands of long black hair. "I think that belongs to the person we've been looking for, and if I'm not mistaken, it's from the woman who's been seen several times. I bet this was also Angel's person in the garden!"

"Finally, a decent clue! It's a big jump to say this is the same person Jerry mentioned, but we can definitely get the DNA from this." Rob took a vial from his pocket and put on gloves.

Meanwhile, Maddie got down on her hands and knees. She followed the rock, rustling through the bracken a little at a time.

"What else are you looking for?" Rob asked over her shoulder.

"Pointing to the rock because that's where Marcus was killed is one thing, but I think there's more. I think there's something else he wants us to find it."

"Us?"

She heard his disbelief, but it didn't perturb her. "I meant, anyone. Or perhaps a member of his family."

A head peered over the rock, and Maddie bit back a scream.

"Sorry. Did I startle you?"

"Dinah. What are you doing here?"

"I needed a walk after all that food." She came around the boulder. "I saw the two of you headed in here, and I have to admit, I was darn curious."

Maddie looked at Rob, who shrugged.

"We're looking for something," Maddie explained.

Dinah's face lit up. "I'm excellent at finding things. What does it look like?"

Nonplussed, Maddie stood. "Umm."

"It's not this, is it?" Dinah bent to pick something up from beside her foot.

"Stop!" Rob shouted.

Poor Dinah clutched her throat and leaned against the rock for support.

Maddie put a hand out to steady her. "It's okay. Detective Jacobs needs us to be careful in case it's evidence for a case."

"Evidence?" Dinah looked down at her feet. "This phone?"

Maddie grinned at Rob. "This very phone. Thanks so much for your help."

Dinah flushed with pride. "I'm so glad I could."

"Could you keep it between us, please?" Rob asked politely, turning a plastic bag inside out and scooping up the phone in a practiced way.

"Well, of course. This is so exciting," Dinah exclaimed.

Rob stood and motioned to Maddie. "We need to get this to the sheriff."

"I understand." Dinah walked with them back to the path on Plum Place. "Good luck."

"We'll talk soon, ma'am." Rob tipped his hat.

Maddie waved, while inside she was brimming with excitement. Was this the clue that could tie everything together?

Chapter Twenty-Four

Gran looked relieved when Maddie walked through the door, and after an expectant look, hugged her. "That didn't take too long," she said softly.

Maddie didn't get a chance to answer before being surrounded by the Girlz.

"We brought back some of the food for all of you since you didn't get time to eat," Angel told her. "Nobody seems hungry, so we're debating whether to leave."

"You Girlz have been on your feet all day from what I hear," Gran told them. "You must stay for a while at least. I'll make more tea."

Angel stood in front of her. "No way. This is still your birthday. We'll take care of refreshments."

Gran knew when she was beaten and sat down in her upright chair. Next to her, William and Ava were on the couch holding hands.

"I wish you'd lie down," Ava told him, fussing with a throw.

"I'd rather sit with the family and enjoy what's left of your mom's day," William told her kindly.

"Did Ethan come back yet?" Maddie asked hopefully.

Gran eyed her thoughtfully. "We haven't heard from anyone."

Disappointed, Maddie curled up on the chaise with Big Red, who'd come out from under the table still looking bloated.

"You look pleased with yourself." Suzy handed Maddie a cup of tea.

"I'm hopeful." She winked.

Ava suddenly looked down at herself and grimaced. "I hadn't realized I was covered in blood. Maybe I'll go have a shower, if you'll be okay?" she asked William.

"With all these women fussing over me, I'm sure to be fine," he said with a grin.

After all he'd been through, William's good humor was undeniable, and Maddie could see what her mom saw in him. That and how much he was devoted to her.

Ava kissed his hand, then placed her cup on the counter before trudging up the stairs.

Big Red pushed off Maddie's lap and stared at the front door. It opened to reveal Nicholas and behind him, Ethan.

"You shouldn't be here," William growled.

Nicholas grimaced. "Where should I be? Back in England with my tail between my legs because you country bumpkins jump to conclusions?"

"You get away from my husband!" Ava roared at him from the bottom of the stairs.

"I'm trying to keep him safe."

"That's my job now."

Nicholas shook his head. "You've known him a couple of months. In that time there's been nothing but drama!"

Ava gasped.

"How dare you speak to my wife this way!" William stood, shaking with anger.

Gran squeezed between all of them. "Either explain things civilly or get out of my house."

Nicholas blinked several times. "You'll listen to me?"

Gran nodded. "We will. Take a seat."

"But. . . ," Ava protested.

"We need to hear him out. With no promises." Gran put her arm through the crooks of Ava's and Maddie's and pulled them into the dining room. "William, sit down before you fall, dear."

William, incapable of further argument, half sat, half fell onto the couch. Ava was by his side in a flash.

Nicholas raised an eyebrow as if he couldn't believe the outcome of his forced visit. Then after waiting for them all to be seated, he sat at the dining table too. Ava's mutinous expression was directed at him, and he scowled right back.

"It's clear that there's no love lost between you two, and I'd like to know the real reason, but first tell us why you've come here, Nicholas," Gran asked, hands folded in front of her.

The man in front of them crumpled. "More accurately, I was brought here by the sheriff. I had no choice about coming today, because I needed to warn William. I didn't kill Marcus. All my attempts to draw out the real murderer have come to nothing, and I didn't know what else to do."

Ava made a rude noise. "Hurting your brother was part of that plan?"

He covered his face with his hands. "I wouldn't have had to do that if he'd simply listened."

William groaned. "Really? Well, it seems you have your wish. I'm a captive audience."

Nicholas grimaced. "You're my brother. You were safer with me than anyone."

"So safe that he almost died in California," Ava pointed out.

"Again, that was your fault. William told me that the drink was yours. Therefore the poison was undoubtedly meant for you."

"Oh. I see. If the poison had killed me, then everything would be alright," Ava said through gritted teeth.

Nicholas scrubbed his face with his hands. "That's not what I'm saying."

"You're not really saying anything," Maddie said, equally annoyed.

Nicholas got to his feet and thrust his hands into his pockets. "I have been William's protector for two decades. He might be older, but he has a different perspective of the world. He wants to believe the best in people. Even those who are not worthy of his trust or love." He gave Ava a pointed look.

"You know nothing about me," Ava's voice was like ice.

"I know everything. I made it my job to find out. How you gave up your child. How you ran away to enjoy life. You have no real qualifications, and you've only ever worked in menial jobs."

Ava gasped, and Gran stood, halting Nicholas midstride.

"If you're only here to insult my family, you'd best leave. Now."

Nicholas flinched. "I'm sorry, Mrs. Flynn. It was never my intention to do that. I have come to believe that Ava cares for my brother. Unfortunately, that has no bearing on her being a suitable wife."

"How dare you speak of her this way? My daughter was

devastated at losing her husband, then suffered another blow when her father passed away. They were very close and she never got over it."

Ava glared at Gran, who looked down at her hands, while Maddie's head threatened to explode.

"Husband?" You married my father?" Maddie's voice croaked out her disbelief.

Ava's face flushed, and she began to wring her hands in earnest. "I didn't want anyone to know about it."

The hurt and anger at the deceit poured from Maddie. "Not even your daughter? Why would you keep that from me?"

"Because it was the best and worst time of my life. I loved him, and I didn't want people to know he ran away. From me or you."

"But he did, didn't he?" Nicholas gave his brother an "I told you so" look.

But William didn't seem surprised by any of this. A man she had known for a short time knew more about her mom than Maddie did, and her heart ached.

Meanwhile, Ava shook her head emphatically. "It wasn't like that. We were very much in love. Grandad insisted we were too young to marry, so we eloped." She looked to Gran. "When my parents found us on that Monday, there was a huge argument. Jake said some awful things to them. Things I couldn't believe he would think about them. I told him to leave, which was a huge mistake, but I didn't want him to stay if he couldn't accept them in our lives. He left, and nine months later I had a child but no husband."

"So that's why you were so angry with Gran and Grandad all the time?" Maddie's sadness spilled out.

Ava didn't look at her. "They never liked your father. I guess I blamed them, and I didn't know how to stop."

Gran made an injured sound. "That's not true, dear. He was a nice enough young man, but we felt as though he was only passing through. He always spoke about where he would go next, never about settling down. I know now that might have suited you, but when he never returned, we believed we'd done the right thing." Gran pulled a handkerchief from the pocket of her apron and dabbed the corners of her eyes.

"It doesn't matter now," Ava said flatly. "It's water under the bridge."

Maddie's fingers had been tapping on her thighs all this time. The story answered questions Gran and Ava had refused to answer, but it raised many more. "Tell me, is my father dead or not?"

"A few days later, there was a major accident in the canyon on the other side of Destiny. His bike lay smashed on the rocks below. There was no body found, but he couldn't have survived the fall into the river. It was swollen by heavy rains and running fast," Ava managed to say in a shaking voice.

"But he could be alive," Maddie stated.

Ava bit her lip. "I have his death certificate."

Maddie's mind whirred. From somewhere deep inside her arose the hope that one day she'd find her father. Dormant for more than a decade or so, the notion brought a warmth. There was a chance he could be alive. Then again, it would mean that he had run out, just like everyone thought.

She shook her head to get rid of the fanciful ideas. Right now there was this mystery to deal with. The other Girlz sat at the table staring at her, while Nicholas, who was back in his seat, looked shamefaced.

"So, you've accepted that Mom cares for William and that she didn't try to kill him?"

Nicholas sighed. "I've seen how they are together, and after my own poisoning when she was still in Maple Falls—well, it speaks for itself."

"I know you don't like Mom, but where did this come from? Surely it's not all based on some kind of snobbery?"

"It was the insurance policy, and the closeness with Marcus," he admitted.

Ava's eyes widened. "What insurance policy?"

"You must know William took out a policy the week after the wedding." Nicholas scoffed.

"I know nothing of the sort!" Ava yelled. "William certainly didn't ask my opinion about that. And if you really did research me, then you would know that I never took anything from anyone."

"You had better have a good point, or get out of my sight in a hurry," William glared back at his brother.

Nicholas seemed to shrink. "It was all in the emails I received."

"What emails?" Maddie was lost, yet sensed that this was important to the case. From the corner of her eye, she saw Ethan slip down the hall. He must know what Nicholas was about to reveal, and she had to deduce that Ethan believed it.

Nicholas shook his head sadly. "They said that Ava was after William's money and Marcus was helping her."

William and Ava paled.

"Emails from who? And what did they say?" Maddie demanded.

"I don't know who sent them. I thought I could handle

it. Someone asked for money, otherwise they would expose Ava as a waitress and a woman of dubious morals. William would be a laughing stock as would our family name." Nicholas shifted awkwardly. "I wondered if it was Marcus. We had some business dealings that were. . . not doing well, and he was struggling to keep afloat. I'd loaned him all I could afford, and he didn't want to ask William. This was where my leap about Marcus and Ava came about."

Just as Maddie's head threatened to explode, Big Red suddenly leaped out from under the table and hissed.

A dark-haired woman walked slowly down the inside stairs, a gun tracking across all four of them.

"I never thought you'd actually tell them," she said with a sneer.

Chapter Twenty-Five

"**A**melia?" Eyes popping, Nicholas couldn't have looked more shocked.

"Father." She looked down her nose at him and everyone in the room.

"What are you doing here?" he managed.

"You're supposed to be a bright man. Put two and two together."

Tall and slender, she wore a tailored navy trouser suit. With almost black eyes and hair, she looked exotic.

None of this helped to ease Maddie's worry over the woman's intent to hurt the people she loved. If possible, Amelia was even more smug than Nicholas. Maddie couldn't see a family resemblance, although the mannerisms were so similar. And where in the smoking bacon did Amelia fit into all this?

Nicholas looked decidedly ill, while William suddenly made a strangled sound.

"You killed Marcus?"

He was on his feet with Ava openmouthed beside him. Gran seemed as bewildered as Maddie. The only one getting any satisfaction from this reunion was the gun-toting stranger.

Amelia shrugged. "We had a plan, Uncle William. Marcus ignored it. I had to take steps to ensure all our hard work and patience—mine has admittedly worn thin—comes to fruition."

Wheels turned, and slowly pieces of the puzzle dropped into place for Maddie. "You and Marcus wanted the castle."

"Well, well. The baker is a clever cookie after all," Amelia sneered. "My very proper father wouldn't take it from his brother, even though he wanted it as much as we did."

It wasn't a compliment, and Maddie sniffed. "So you decided to kill everyone in your way. Including your father's uncle, who owned the castle?"

"As much as I'd like to take the credit for his demise, I wasn't even in England. I was over here setting up everything for William and my father. All those terrible business deals wouldn't play out by themselves," Amelia scoffed.

Now that Amelia had pretty much confessed to killing Marcus, Maddie wanted all the truth out so that Ethan could hear. "Why did you try to poison William and your father?"

"Goodness, you ask a lot of questions. And we don't have much time before Jerry wakes up again." Her eyes glinted. "I'll just say that my uncle and my father are very old-fashioned and without my intervention it would be a very long time, if ever, that the castle was mine."

Amelia pointed disdainfully at Ava. "Then William comes here and marries her. A woman who has a child, so now I'm further down the pecking order than before."

Maddie was astonished by this line of thinking, and the brothers looked like they were in pain.

Nicholas groaned at the confession. "I don't understand. You have everything you could ever want. Your mother and I made sure of it."

The gun tilted in Amelia's hands. "Having things is not the same as being loved."

"We both loved you, and yet you tried to poison me. Your own father!"

Nicholas looked as shell-shocked as the other people in the room. Perhaps more so.

The gun snapped up. "Adopted father and that was to keep you out of the picture for a while. Besides, you can't deny that you wanted the castle. We both did."

Maddie licked her lips. Antagonizing Amelia was a bad idea. She had a wild look in her eyes. Maddie could only assume that Ethan was waiting on backup, or maybe it was the way the gun moved from potential targets with incredible frequency that prevented him from making his move.

First, keep them talking. If they talk, they probably won't shoot. Maddie heard Grandad's voice as if he sat next to her.

Heeding his advice, it occurred to Maddie that Marcus had played a bigger part than they'd appreciated. "Marcus helped you, didn't he?"

Amelia paled. "Even Marcus would have gotten the castle before me and he didn't think it was fair either."

"Why would it trouble him? Unless you two were an item?"

"Bravo!" Amelia grinned.

Nicholas put his head in his hands and groaned again. William looked like he'd been kicked in the stomach. Tears rolled down Ava's cheeks.

"You used his affection for you against William?" Maddie asked.

Amelia nodded. "He'd been the poor cousin for so long and I was the adopted child so it was natural that we formed an alliance. Marcus came over here with William to look into a business deal I'd concocted to get him out of the country. I figured once he was isolated, I'd make my move. Then they met the waitress."

Now the gun was aimed at Ava.

"I had to send my father to shut that down, but my dear uncle eloped."

Maddie tried to draw Amelia's attention away from her mom. "And that's when Marcus suddenly got cold feet?"

"We could have had it all, but he was as taken in by the gold digger as his cousin!" Amelia spat the words.

Maddie stood and took miniscule steps toward the couch where her mother and stepfather were. "William loves my mother. You can surely see that?"

Amelia snorted. "He thinks he does. Eloping kind of says he knew my father would be upset about him marrying her." Then she gulped. "I don't know what hold she has over him and I don't care, but she didn't have to weave Marcus into her web."

Ava looked confused and scared in equal measure. Was she wondering, like Maddie and potentially Gran, how truly deranged William's niece was?

Another lightbulb flashed in Maddie's brain. "You were using Marcus to keep anyone from suspecting that you intended to get rid of William and pin it on my mom."

Amelia nodded. "Bingo! It was going to be a win-win situation. Until Marcus fell under her spell. Suddenly, he didn't want to hurt anybody. The simpleton not only mixed up the glasses, he also let slip that he was the one who called for help."

"Did Marcus help Mom get away?"

Amelia's eyes narrowed. "I'm sure he did, but your mother would know for sure."

Ava sobbed into William's chest.

"So you followed Marcus to Maple Falls and killed him." Maddie pulled her attention back from her mom.

Amelia gulped, the only sign that she wasn't totally without remorse. "When I arrived in Destiny, Marcus was threatening to come clean to William. We fought, and I pushed him. He hit his head on a rock. It wasn't my fault."

Nicholas leaned toward his daughter. "You need help. You don't know what you're saying."

She arced the gun around the room once more. "If I kill you all, then no one will be able to pin any of this on me, because no one has seen me but you people."

"You were in my garden!" Angel shouted.

Bizarrely, Amelia laughed. "Everyone thought you were crazy, but I was a star gymnast, so those walls didn't slow me down at all. I'd been amusing myself watching you all at the bakery while I waited for William to show himself."

The woman must be unhinged, which meant that she was capable of killing them all, and Maddie had run out of ideas. She glanced down the hall again. No Ethan. Could she possibly disarm Amelia on her own?

"Well, this has been fun, but I need to get out of town. We all know what that means," Amelia growled. "Father, you have a choice to make. Are you with me or not?"

Nicholas sat straighter. "I could never condone killing anyone, let alone my brother. I don't understand you, Amelia. I love you, and I'm begging you not to ruin your life this way."

The gun wobbled a little, and Amelia seemed less sure of her objective. Maddie gave her friends a pointed look before facing the woman again.

"Do you have enough bullets for all of us, and aren't you worried that someone will hear so many shots?"

The others gave her horrified looks, but Maddie ignored them.

Amelia seemed to sense that Maddie was up to something. She made sure to keep out of Nicholas's reach, circling them to give herself more room and see Maddie, and now her back was to the hall.

"No one's around. You live on a small farm, and there are fields around you. So convenient," Amelia chuckled.

Maddie frowned, as if giving that some thought. "What about the shops? People live above the block of four where my bakery is. They're not so far from here."

Amelia stared at her. "I doubt anyone will think it more than a car backfiring."

"Several times?"

Amelia shot Gran's easy chair. A hole pierced the fabric and lodged in the wall behind it. "Shut up! You're giving me a headache."

Ava's scream led the following pandemonium. William threw himself in front of his wife. From the top of the dresser, a ginger ball launched itself and landed on Amelia's head. She wailed, the gun clattering to the floor when she reached both hands up to pull Big Red free and throw him from her. Hackles up, making a horrible sound, he slid a few feet before darting under the table.

Heart in her mouth, Maddie yelled something unintelligible and kicked the gun away from Amelia. Nicholas stood, but seemed incapable of doing more.

"Stay where you are!"

Maddie could have wept in palpable relief as Amelia swung to face Ethan. He'd slipped from the mud room and down the hall, as quiet as a mouse.

Then the front door swung open. It banged and reverberated against the wall as Detective Steve Jones ran into the room. He stood in front of the group, his gun also trained on Amelia.

Outnumbered and outmaneuvered, Amelia paled, her hands in the air. In the slickest of movements, Ethan snapped cuffs on her wrists.

"I'm not a U.S. citizen," she said lamely.

Ethan raised an eyebrow. "That's true, but it bears no relevance to the fact that you committed several crimes while in our country, and I heard you admit to all of them."

Ethan placed a hand under Amelia's elbow and marched the shocked woman past the people she'd terrorized. When he got to the door, he handed her over to Deputy Jacobs, who took her outside.

"I'm so sorry," William said softly to the room at large.

"It's I who should apologize," Nicholas said, his face awash with tears. "How could I have been so blind?"

No one answered, and as much as Maddie disliked how he'd treated her mom, her heart ached for him.

"What will they do with her?" Nicholas asked.

"My deputies are taking her to our cells for the night. Tomorrow she'll go on to Destiny, where she'll face a trial. I can't say how long that will take, but there will no doubt be prison time," Ethan explained.

Ava leaned her head against William's shoulder. "I'm sure you can afford a good lawyer to get her home as soon as possible."

He kissed her forehead and managed a trembling smile. "You are a remarkable woman, Mrs. Blackwell."

C. A. Phipps

Ava flushed. "I just know how much you love family, and even Amelia killing Marcus won't change the fact you feel somehow responsible."

He kissed her again, and Maddie took the opportunity to hug Gran. It was over. Nothing she'd imagined came close to how this had turned out. She had more family than she'd thought possible—some not so good—and William was proving to be everything Ava had hinted at. Her mom was also proving to have more to her than Maddie had thought.

Leaving William to console his brother, Ava came to join her mother and daughter in a hug that was both alien and natural. Maddie could barely breathe, but she didn't care. They were all safe.

"Where does this leave us?" Nicholas asked.

William shrugged. "In the same situation, I guess."

Ava pulled away from the group hug to tap William's arm. "I've been thinking about that, dear."

His voice became instantly softer. "Yes, my love?"

"I have no need of a castle, and you don't care if you live there or not. Why don't you and Nicholas swap places?"

William's eyes widened. "Swap? Well, I don't know about that. It wouldn't look right," he blustered.

Ava raised an eyebrow. "Do you care so much what people think of you, especially after this fiasco?"

"Not the majority of people, but there are our peers," William admitted.

"Will they think less of you for not living in a castle when you have an estate to run? Won't Nicholas become their focus, and you could live more peacefully?"

William rested his hand on Ava's hip and drew her close. "Is this truly what you want?"

"I want whatever makes you happy, and I'll live wherever you choose, but Nicholas wants the castle so badly. He

210

has tried to protect you. In his own stupid way and from the wrong people."

William stared hard at his brother. "He didn't try to protect you, though. I don't know if I can forgive him for that."

Ava cupped his chin and made him meet her eyes. "Yes, you can. He's your brother and, unfortunately, your only living relative who isn't incarcerated."

He frowned. "Do you forgive him?"

"I didn't think I could, but now that I've heard his story and see how passionate he is about the castle and your family name, I think he should have his dreams fulfilled. After all, it was only a fluke of birth that he didn't get it in the first place." Ava sighed. "It will be hard enough having his daughter behind bars and knowing it was she who killed Marcus."

"And could have killed either one of us." William noted as he turned to his brother. "We used to be so close."

Nicholas looked distraught and awkward, not at all like the self-righteous man he'd portrayed. "I no longer know what to say, except I'm sorry." His voice choked with emotion. "I knew Amelia was having anger issues. To be honest, she'd been troubled for many years. I should have looked into them more instead of pretending they didn't exist."

"We all wish you had. Still, I'm glad that you weren't involved. Maybe Ava's right about the castle, but I'd have to look into the legalities." William stared hard at his brother. "And from this moment, you will treat my wife with every respect."

The cloud over Nicholas seemed to lift a little. He nodded effusively. "I don't deserve this, and you have my word. Ava has proven that she is a much better person than I could hope to be."

Gran sat down in her chair, looking every one of her seventy years. "Don't fuss," she said to the Girlz who crowded around her. "Now that things are more or less settled, I'll take a moment to calm down and then I'm off to bed."

Maddie nodded, understanding how she must feel, since her own legs were decidedly wobbly. She looked around the room, feeling incredibly relieved. Then she frowned. "Where's Laura?"

"Behind you." Suzy grinned. "Poor thing fainted as soon as she saw the gun."

"I'm okay, just a bit woozy," Laura said from where she sat on the floor.

"You poor thing. I'm sorry I didn't notice."

From behind her, Ethan took her arm. "I believe you were otherwise engaged." He pulled her into the kitchen and into his arms. "You never listen to me, do you?"

She smiled and put a hand on his cheek. "When it counts."

He grinned and kissed her. Suzy couldn't help herself, as a small whoop from the other room made them more prudent.

"How did you know Amelia was in the house?"

"Steve's been here since before you got back. He messaged me after I brought in Nicholas to say a woman had been spotted climbing in an upstairs window. Then Jerry was found outside wandering around in a daze and that kept the other's busy for a few minutes."

"I wondered what was taking you so long," she teased.

He grimaced. "Without help I didn't know how we

were going to get everyone out safely. It scared the life out of me."

Maddie nodded, appreciating his anguish. "Me too." Suddenly she was overwhelmed with emotion and dabbed the corner of her eyes. "So many secrets, half-truths, and a touch of crazy in one room. I felt completely out of my depth."

Ethan cupped her chin. "It certainly didn't look like it, and you had your sidekick to help." "He nodded at Big Red who appeared no worse for his ninja-like tactics. "Besides, this was a harder case than usual to untangle. Getting Amelia to fire the gun that way was genius, if a little foolhardy."

She snorted. "I think I went a little crazy too."

He grinned again. "I got Rob's message about the phone. Now, that was brilliant detective work."

She shrugged. "We couldn't access any messages yet, but it was Marcus's so I'm sure there's good information on it."

"Hopefully, but at least you solved the riddle of the pointing finger."

The glow from his praise warmed her heart and as he held her tight Maddie relished the feeling of safety.

Chapter Twenty-Six

When they joined the rest of the group, Detective Jones was about to leave.

"You did a good job today, Madeline."

She blushed at the praise. "It was a team effort."

"Finding that phone could make all the difference to the case in confirming or refuting what Ms. Blackwell told us."

Maddie shook her head. "That part wasn't really me. We have Mrs. Dolomore to thank for that. Her keen eyes picked it out of all the undergrowth when I missed it."

"I don't know her, and I'll make a point of thanking her, but this was more than finding a phone. Perhaps you should think about a change of career?"

Surprised, Maddie laughed at the outrageous comment. "No, thank you. I'm happy being an ordinary baker in a quiet town."

"Hmmm. I don't think you'll ever be just that." The detective grinned for a moment. "Mr. Blackwell, are you ready?"

"Yes, and thanks for the ride. I need to check on Amelia," he said to them all, but was looking at William.

"Of course you must. We'll talk soon." William shook his brother's hand.

With a final apologetic glance around the room, Nicholas left.

Steve Jones bid them all goodnight, and after a nod to Angel he followed.

Maddie felt so good right then, but there was more to come.

"I'm so proud of you." Ava smiled happily. "I knew you were the right person to help. You're so much braver than me."

Maddie's eyes welled. "I'm glad you trusted me. And I'm glad you came home and brought new family." If her mom could forgive Nicholas, then she should take a leaf out of her book. As for being brave, Maddie decided that her mom might have passed on a few of those genes.

William kissed her cheek. "Thank you. I'm delighted to be a part of three wonderful and beautiful generations of Flynns. We'll certainly miss you and your friends. If you're ever over in our neck of the woods, you should come for a visit, anytime you feel the urge."

Maddie nodded. A trip to England? That sounded amazing. "I'd like to drive you to the airport, if that's okay?"

He smiled. "You've done enough. We can take a taxi."

Maddie shook her head. "I'd like to see you for a little longer without all the chaos around us. Maybe chat about that trip?" she teased.

Ava looked to her husband, who nodded. "Then we'd love that too."

Maddie heard the truth in her mom's voice.

"Perhaps you could rustle us up something to eat?" William gently asked his wife when his stomach growled.

Maddie gasped at the request, but her mom didn't appear put out. "You cook?"

Her mother raised both eyebrows. "No need to sound so surprised. I lived with Gran until I was nearly nineteen. Naturally, I picked up a thing or two."

"Your mom was a very good cook. She would stand at the kitchen counter just like you did and bake beside me," Gran noted wistfully.

Maddie turned to her mom. "I didn't know that."

Ava shrugged. "I guess you only saw the bad things I did."

Gran tutted. "I promise that I told Maddie about all the fun times we had. You, me, and your father."

"I'm glad she got to have that too. I've never said how much I appreciated Maddie was well looked after and loved. It helped with the guilt." Ava's mouth trembled.

"This is turning sad. How about someone gets in the kitchen?" Suzy's watery eyes conflicted with her firm voice. "Besides, there's so much food here, no one needs to cook!"

"Well, I'm starved," Angel admitted.

They all laughed, even William. Angel's love of food was spreading. Ava shook her head and with a grin headed to the kitchen, waving away Gran, who had stood.

"You take it easy for once, Mom," Ava told her.

A sniff had all eyes turning to Gran. Tears rolled down her face, and Maddie enveloped her in her arms. "What's wrong?"

Gran looked to the kitchen, joy flowing from her like the tears. "Don't mind me. I'm a silly fool who, despite such appalling things happening, is just so happy she could burst."

"You're not old, and you're certainly no fool," Ava

called from the kitchen. She wore a broad smile as she donned one of Gran's aprons.

The world shifted beneath Maddie, and she hugged Gran closer. It seemed that everyone could change and the world wasn't black and white. What you knew and what you assumed could also be born in lies you told yourself.

The house buzzed with conversation. This was family. A hotchpotch of blood relatives and those who behaved as though they were.

Maddie wouldn't have it any other way, and neither would Big Red, who meandered through the crowd, accepting tidbits until he looked as though he would burst. Again.

Eventually, he lay under the table, keeping half-closed eyes on his family.

Thanks so much for reading Eclairs and Extortion. I hope you enjoyed it!

If you did...
1 Help other people find this book by leaving a review.

2 Sign up for my new release e-mail, so you can find out about the next book as soon as it's available.

3 Come like my Facebook page.

4 Visit my website for the very best deals.

5 Keep reading for an excerpt from Fudge and Frenemies.

Fudge and Frenemies

They climbed the majestic staircase which opened up to a hall where rows of portraits hung in orderly lines. Opposite these, the group looked over the railing to the floor below. With this second amazing perspective, Maddie fell in love with the castle. It was a shame that it would be given to William's brother, but her stepfather and Ava seemed happy with the decision.

Her mom waited patiently for them to finish gawping

before heading to the right. "Our rooms are in the other wing and yours are down here."

They walked a long way before Ava stopped in front of the first door and opened it. "Mom, this is your suite."

Excitedly, Gran walked into the small sitting room. Beyond this was a bedroom. "A whole suite? For me?"

Angel ran around the rooms like a headless chicken, exclaiming over everything. "The size of this is crazy! Come, look at the bed—it's a four poster. I love this suite. Oh, my—the furniture is Georgian. Sugar, you have to see the bathroom! A clawed bath and gold taps."

"Calm down, Angel. There's plenty more to see but you might have a heart attack at this rate," Ava laughed. "Mom, your bags are here already, so you can freshen up and have a nap if you want. A gong will sound at 7 p.m. when dinner is served in the main dining room. Girls, come with me."

Gran's case was indeed on a stand in her room and she winked at them. "I guess I could rest a while. See you at 7."

Next stop was Angel's room where they were forced to endure a similar scenario, and then again when they reached Maddie's which was back down the corridor opposite Gran's room.

Maddie explored her suite more slowly. "Mom, this place is amazing and the furniture is incredible."

Ava grinned. "I never appreciated old things until I came here. This stuff is so well looked after, and beautifully made, I confess to being a little in love with every piece."

Maddie couldn't remember a time when Ava enthusiastic over anything except escaping their hometown of Maple Falls—and lately William. She literally sparkled and seemed younger when she spoke about her new home. England obviously agreed with her. Stifling a yawn, Maddie tried to hide her jet-lag but Ava noticed.

"You'll be tired after that flight too. I know because it took me several days to get over it. Since you're only here for a twelve days, I hope it won't take you so long, but maybe you should take a nap too. We can talk later."

"It doesn't feel right to turn up and go to bed, and I do want to hear all your news, but I am shattered. There was so much to do before I left. Will you wake us if we oversleep?"

Ava glanced at Angel before nodding. "I won't need to —you'll hear the gong, trust me. Now, I'll leave the two of you to unpack and at least relax. Come to the main dining room when you're ready."

"What was that about?" Angel asked the minute the door closed.

"What do you mean?"

"Your mom clearly has something on her mind. I'm sorry if I was in the way."

"We do have a lot to talk about but I'm sure a few hours won't hurt."

"Well, I know you two need to reconnect so don't hold back if you need me to vamoose at any time, Sugar."

"You can count on it," Maddie teased, relieved that her friend was so understanding.

"I should unpack, otherwise everything will be creased beyond recognition." Angel went back to her room but was back ten minutes later. "I've unpacked, now what?"

"Aren't you tired?" Maddie put the last of her clothes in the ornate dresser with a sigh.

Flopping down on the sofa, Angel put her hands behind her head. "There'll be time to be tired later. I want to see it all."

"I guarantee everything will still be here when we wake up," Maddie assured her.

"What if it's just a dream?"

"Then anything you see won't count, will it?" Maddie laughed as she stood by the French doors and took in the sight of the garden below the floor to ceiling windows. "I admit that this trip is surreal and a little crazy how it came about so quickly."

"Absolutely, but a pretty cool kinda crazy, Sugar. We didn't have time to fret as much as usual about leaving our businesses in other people's care."

"You're right, and I do want to explore, but I'm so tired. If I ventured out you'd be carrying me back."

"That's not happening." Angel wrinkled her nose. "I guess I could lay down for half an hour if I must."

"You don't know how relieved I am to hear it. How about we start the in-depth exploration first thing tomorrow?"

"Count me in." Angel dragged herself up and left, closing the door behind her.

Maddie looked longingly at the bath in the adjoining bathroom, but her eyes were already drooping. After a quick shower she put on pajamas—the ones with *Garfield* which reminded her of her of Big Red. Then she climbed under the softest of covers and in between the crispest of sheets.

"Just an hour or two," she promised herself, almost convinced that Big Red was snuggled at her back.

A sound above her, like someone moving furniture almost pulled her awake but it stopped as suddenly as it began and she burrowed under the blanket. Old homes and castle's in particular would have odd noises. Right?

Need to read more?
Pick up your copy of Fudge and Frenemies today!

Recipes

These recipes are ones I use all the time and have come down the generations from my mum, grandmother, and some I have adapted from other recipes.

Also, I am now in possession of my husband's grandmother's recipe book. Exciting! I'll be bringing some of them to life very soon.

Just a wee reminder, that I am a New Zealander. Occasionally, I may have missed converting into ounces and pounds for my American readers.

My apologies for that, and please let me know, if you do try them, how they turn out.

Keep well.
Cheryl x

Eclairs

Ingredients

75g (5 tbsp.) butter
1 cup water
1 cup of plain baking flour
2 teaspoons sugar
1/2 tsp vanilla essence
3 eggs
whipped cream
chocolate frosting

Instructions

Heat oven to 200°C / 390°F
Line baking tray with baking paper.
In a saucepan, bring butter and water to the boil.
Add flour and beat rapidly with a wooden spoon until mixture forms a ball.
Remove from heat.
Add sugar and vanilla, then add eggs one at a time, beating well after each one.

Place mixture into a piping bag with a large nozzle and pipe into strips onto baking paper.

Bake for 30 minutes or until they are golden.

Cool.

Using a sharp knife poke a hole from one end through to the other.

Fill with whipped cream and then frost.

Chocolate Frosting

Ingredients

2 cups of confectioners' sugar

1 tbsp. cocoa

1/4 tsp butter

2 tbsps. water

Instructions

Sift sugar and cocoa.

Blend in butter.

Add enough water to mix to a honey-like consistency.

Gingernuts

(Makes 2 dozen)

Ingredients

125g (4 1/2 ozs) butter
1/4 cup brown sugar
3 tbsps. maple syrup
2 cups plain flour
pinch of salt
1 tsp baking soda
2 tsp ground ginger
1 tbsp. boiling water

Instructions

Heat oven to at 180°C / 350°F.

Cream butter, sugar, and syrup in a bowl until light and fluffy.

Dissolve baking soda in the boiling water.

Add to creamed mixture.

Sift flour, salt, and ginger together.

Add to creamed mixture, mixing well.

Rolled tablespoons of mixture into balls and onto the tray.

Flatten with a fork.

Bake for 20 to 30 minutes until golden.

Also by C. A. Phipps

Midlife Potions - Paranormal Cozy Mysteries

Witchy Awakening

Witchy Hot Spells

Witchy Flash Back

Witchy Bad Blood - preorder now!

The Cozy Café Mysteries

Sweet Saboteur

Candy Corruption

Mocha Mayhem

Berry Betrayal

Deadly Double-Dip

The Maple Lane Cozy Mysteries

Sugar and Sliced - Maple Lane Prequel

Apple Pie and Arsenic

Bagels and Blackmail

Cookies and Chaos

Doughnuts and Disaster

Eclairs and Extortion

Fudge and Frenemies

Gingerbread and Gunshots

Honey Cake and Homicide - preorder now!

Beagle Diner Cozy Mysteries

Beagles Love Cupcake Crimes

Beagles Love Steak Secrets

Beagles Love Muffin But Murder

Beagles Love Layer Cake Lies

Please note: Most are also available in paperback and some in audio.

Remember to join Cheryl's Cozy Mystery newsletter.

There's a free recipe book waiting for you. ;-)

Cheryl also writes romance as Cheryl Phipps.

About the Author

'Life is a mystery. Let's follow the clues together.'

C. A. Phipps is a USA Today best-selling author from beautiful New Zealand. Cheryl lives in a quiet suburb with her wonderful husband, whom she married the moment she left school (yes, they were high school sweethearts). With three married children and seven grandchildren to keep her busy when she's not writing, there is just enough space for a crazy mixed breed dog who stole her heart! She enjoys family times, baking, rambling walks, and her quest for the perfect latte.

Check out her website http://caphipps.com

facebook.com/authorcaphipps
x.com/CherylAPhipps
instagram.com/caphippsauthor

Made in the USA
Middletown, DE
18 August 2024

59390260R00142